SUGAR ISLAND GIRL

MISSING IN PARIS

A number of very wonderful people helped me prepare this book for publication. Each of them contributed significantly. Thank you Evie, Meredith, and Charity. And special thanks to George and Gay.

SUGAR ISLAND GIRL

MISSING IN PARIS

MICHAEL CARRIER

GREENWICH VILLAGE INK

GRAND RAPIDS, MICHIGAN

SUGAR ISLAND GIRL—MISSING IN PARIS

Published 2014 by Greenwich Village Ink, Grand Rapids, MI.

Visit the JACK website at http://www.greenwichvillageink.com/
For additional information (and sometimes puzzles) visit JACK's blog: http://jackhandlerny.blogspot.com/.

Author can be emailed at mike.jon.carrier@gmail.com. You can follow Michael's tweets at @MikeCarrier999.

ISBN: 978-1-936092-33-8 (trade pbk)
Printed in the United States of America

Library of Congress Cataloging-in-Publication Data

Carrier, Michael.
SUGAR ISLAND GIRL, Missing in Paris / by Michael Carrier. 1st ed.
ISBN: 978-1-936092-33-8 (trade pbk. : alk. paper)
1. Hard Boiled Thriller 2. Mystery 3. Thriller 4. Novel 5. Murder 6. Burglary 7. New York. 8. Michigan's Upper Peninsula. 7. Paris.

Contents

What people are saying about the "Getting to Know Jack" series

Finally, there is a new author who will challenge the likes of Michael Connelly and David Baldacci. — Island Books

If you like James Patterson and Michael Connelly, you'll love Michael Carrier. Carrier has proven that he can hang with the best of them. It has all of the great, edge-of-your-seat action and suspense that you'd expect in a good thriller, and it kept me guessing to the very end. Fantastic read with an awesome detective duo—I couldn't put it down! — Katie

Don't read Carrier at the beach or you are sure to get sunburned. I did. I loved the characters. It was so descriptive you feel like you know everyone. Lots of action—always something happening. I love the surprise twists. All my friends are reading it now because I wouldn't talk to them until I finished it so they knew it was good. Carrier is my new favorite author! — Sue

Thoroughly enjoyed this read — kept me turning page after page! Good character development and captivating plot. Had theories but couldn't quite solve the mystery without reading to the end. Highly recommended for readers of all ages. — Terry

Top Shelf Murder Mystery—Riveting. Being a Murder-Mystery "JUNKIE" this book is definitely a keeper ... can't put it down ... read it again type of book...and it is very precise to the lifestyles in Upper Michigan. Very well researched. I am a resident of this area. His attention to detail is great. I have to rate this book in the same class or better than authors Michael Connelly, James Patterson, and Steve Hamilton. — Shelldrakeshores

Being a Michigan native, I was immediately drawn to this book. Michael Carrier is right in step with his contemporaries James Patterson and David Baldacci. I am anxious to read more of his work. I highly recommend this one! — J. Henningsen

A fast and interesting read. Michael ends each chapter with a hook that makes you want to keep reading. The relationship between father and daughter is compelling. Good book for those who like a quick moving detective story where the characters often break the "rules" for the greater good! I'm looking forward to reading the author's next book. — Flower Lady

Move over Patterson, I now have a new favorite author, Jack and his daughter make a great tag team, great intrigue, and diversions. I have a cabin on Sugar Island and enjoyed the references to the locations. I met the author at Joey's coffee shop up on the hill, (the real live Joey) great writer, good stuff. I don't usually finish a book in the course of a week, but read this one in two sittings so it definitely had my attention. I am looking forward to the next installment. Bravo. — Northland Press

My husband is not a reader— he probably hasn't read a book since his last elementary school book report was due. But ... he took my copy of Murder on Sugar Island to deer camp and read the whole thing in two days. After he recommended the book to me, I read it— being the book snob that I am, I thought I had the whole plot figured out within the first few pages, but a few chapters later, I was mystified once again. After that surprise ending, we ordered the other two Getting to Know Jack books. — Erin W.

I enjoyed this book very much. It was very entertaining, and the story unfolded in a believable manner. Jack Handler is a likable character. But you would not like to be on his wrong side. Handler made that very clear in Jack and the New York Death Mask. This book (Murder on Sugar Island) was the first book in the Getting to Know Jack series that I read. After I read Death Mask, I discovered just how tough Jack Handler really was.

I heard that Carrier is about to come out with another Jack Handler book—a sequel to Superior Peril. I will read it the day it becomes available. And I will undoubtedly finish it before I go to bed. If he could write them faster, I would be happy.

Actually, I'll take what I can get. — Deborah M.

I thoroughly enjoyed this book. I could not turn the pages fast enough. I am not sure it was plausible, but I love the characters. I highly recommend this book and look forward to reading more by Michael Carrier. — Amazon Reader

An intense thrill ride!! — Mario

Michael Carrier has knocked it out of the park — John

Left on the edge of my seat after the last book, I could not wait for the next chapter to unfold and Mike Carrier did not disappoint! I truly feel I know his characters better with each novel and I especially like the can-do/will-do attitude of Jack. Keep up the fine work, Mike and may your pen never run dry! — SW

The Handlers are at it again, with the action starting on Sugar Island, I am really starting to enjoy the way the father, daughter and now Red are working through the mind of Mike Carrier. The entire family, plus a few more, are becoming the reason for the new sheriff's increased body count and antacid intake. The twists and turns we have come to expect are all there and then some. I'm looking for the next installment already. — Northland Press

Preface

If you enjoy this book you should consider writing a short five-star review on Amazon (http://amzn.to/1t9R9r9). It is not required that you have purchased the book from Amazon, only that you have an account. It will be greatly appreciated.

SUGAR ISLAND GIRL, MISSING IN PARIS (MISSING) is the fifth part of the "Getting to Know Jack" series. All print books in the series can be purchased through Amazon and from select bookstores, and all are available as eBooks through the Amazon Kindle Bookstore.

The first book of the series is entitled *JACK AND THE NEW YORK DEATH MASK (JACK)*. Two of the three main characters of the series (Jack and Kate Handler) were introduced in JACK.

MURDER ON SUGAR ISLAND (SUGAR) is part two of the "Getting to Know Jack" series.

SUPERIOR PERIL (PERIL) is the third book of the series, and *SUPERIOR INTRIGUE* is the fourth.

For a more thorough summary of the backstory, check the Cast of Characters section at the back of this book.

DISCLAIMER: None of the books in the "Getting to Know Jack" series represent true stores—they are all works of fiction. All characters, names, situations, and occurrences are purely the product of the author's imagination. Any resemblance to actual events, or persons (living or dead), is totally coincidental.

For additional information visit Jack's page on the publisher's website, http://www.greenwichvillageink.com/.

The author, Michael Carrier, holds a Master of Arts degree from New York University, and has worked in private security for over two decades.

Chapter 1

Sunday, 4:00 a.m. Sugar Island time

(A short back-story is included in the "Cast of Characters" section at the end of this book)

Whadda we got here?" the desk sergeant groaned. It was four in the morning on a Sunday. Sergeant James Lawrence (JL) Gordon had worked all night dealing with the Saturday night regulars, and he did not want to be bothered with any more late arrivals.

"He was driving under the influence," Deputy Hopkins said.

"And he's a genuine *troll*. License says he's from Detroit."

Those who live in the Upper Peninsula of Michigan commonly refer to those from the Lower Peninsula as trolls—in other words, creatures that live under (or south of) the Mackinac Bridge. It is, of course, intended as an innocuous pejorative.

"What's his name?" JL asked. "Or better yet, does he have friends in the city? Someone who might be so kind as to come and take him off our hands?"

"No. He said he was on his way back home," Deputy Hopkins replied. "His driver's license says he is one David Russell Hughes."

"Lucky me," the sergeant said. "Couldn't you have just escorted him out of town? Wasn't there something you could do besides bring him to me? Anything?"

"We don't do stuff like that. Besides, he's got a story the boss is gonna want to hear … right away."

"What's this 'we don't do stuff like that' bullshit? Look, once I snap his picture, we're gonna have to process him. Isn't there something you can do to get him outta our hair?"

Deputy Hopkins was not paying attention to his grumbling.

JL took a long look at the prisoner standing in front of him. The man appeared to be in his early forties. His expensive designer jeans and tan button-down shirt stood out, but it was the black Armani Collezioni leather bomber jacket that really looked out of place in the Upper Peninsula, much less in a holding cell.

JL lined him up for his mug shot and snapped it.

"Six feet three inches—you're a tall one," JL mumbled.

The prisoner did not acknowledge the comment.

There was something about this guy that JL found striking, but it had little to do with his height or his clothes. It was mostly in the manner he handled his steely dark eyes. He had a way of looking past you, instead of at you. Deep creases between his brows accented further the power of his stare, giving him the appearance of intense constant preoccupation.

And he did not respond verbally to directives; he merely did as he was told in a supremely stoic fashion.

JL noticed that the handcuffs appeared to be cutting off the prisoner's circulation, so he examined them to be sure no damage could result. *These hands do not belong to a working man,* he thought. As he was satisfying himself that the cuffs were tight, but not overly so, he observed a two-digit number tattooed on the inside of the right wrist.

"Prison ink, right? Where did you do your time?"

Again the prisoner did not respond.

"There's nothin' the old man wants right now except to sleep it off," JL said. "If you know what I mean. I heard he closed up Moloney's last night … this morning, actually. He can't be feelin' so hot right now."

"He's gonna want a call, trust me," Hopkins said. "You call him, or I will. But he needs to hear this guy's story. And, by the way, make a note on your form that the prisoner has a bandage below his right ear—an *existing* minor injury."

"Fine, then you call the sheriff," JL said, tossing a pair of slip-on booties at the prisoner.

"Lose those fancy shoes, *and* the jacket," he said. "The boys in the back will have a field day with you if they see any of that stuff."

JL then handed the prisoner a basket for his personal belongings.

"Looks like you know the drill, partner," JL said. "You get

locked up a lot?"

The prisoner did not respond; he just slipped his black Forzieri Italian handcrafted leather cap-toe shoes into the metal basket and then carefully folded his jacket and placed it on top of the shoes.

"Exactly what is it you need to tell the old man?" JL asked.

"I'll talk only to the sheriff," the prisoner said, not looking at JL.

"Fine then, have it your way," JL snorted back. "But don't count on our sheriff cutting you any breaks. That's not how it works around here. I'll just get you processed. And then you can go back and get acquainted with new best friends."

"The sheriff says to just put our buddy in an interrogation room until he gets here," Deputy Hopkins said.

"Then the old man's coming down here?"

"He sure is."

"What exactly is it that this fellow wants to tell the sheriff?"

Deputy Hopkins waited until two officers had escorted the prisoner back to an interrogation room before responding. And then he said, "I think he might be the dealer who supplied that guy with heroin. You know, that Reginald Black guy—the one that OD'd a week or two ago. Well, he suggested to me that it wasn't an *accidental* overdose—that somebody wanted the guy killed, and that he, this Hughes guy, might even have taken part in it."

"Really! He says it was *murder*?"

"That's right, and he said he's willing to make a deal. But *only* with the sheriff. My guess is he's goin' in for a long time with any kind of conviction. You know, because of his record. And he desperately wants to avoid that."

"He looks more like a pimp than a dealer to me," JL commented. "I don't know much about fancy clothes like that, but I'd guess he was sporting a couple grand, at least."

"You're just jealous."

"Hardly," JL replied. "Where'd I wear that coat, or those shoes? Anyway, when's the old man gonna get here? After I've gone home, I hope."

"I don't think so," Hopkins said. "He sounded pretty excited to me. I'd bet he walks through that door in the next five minutes."

"I hope he ain't driving," JL said. "He's gotta be drunk on his ass."

"I'm *sure* he's driving," Deputy Hopkins chuckled. "And I think it'd be a really great career move on your part were you to share that opinion with the sheriff—the part about him being drunk on his ass. I'm sure he'd like to hear your view on that."

Looking down at his paperwork, JL did not crack a smile at Deputy Hopkins's humor.

JL had been with the department for the past six years. He was well liked by the community and by his superiors but was impatient at times with what he perceived to bc Deputy Hopkins's inappropriate behavior and occasional failure to respect authority.

JL had tried to keep the night shift professional, making sure all of the regulations were followed. He felt that sometimes Hopkins came off like a real jerk to witnesses and detainees, as well as to other officers. JL made mental notes of this inappropriate behavior, thinking that someday the boss might want to know exactly how things were handled when he was not there to supervise.

Only a few moments had passed when Sheriff Green bolted through the door.

"Where's the prisoner?" he demanded.

"Follow me," JL said, as he headed down the dimly lit hallway toward where the officers had deposited the prisoner.

"Room A or B?" the sheriff demanded, pushing past the sergeant.

"B," JL replied. "A is in use right now."

When the sheriff looked through the one-way glass in the door he shouted, "What the hell is this!"

Alone inside interrogation room B, on the floor beside a stainless steel table and overturned stainless steel chair, with his hands still securely cuffed, lying in a growing pool of blood, twitched the body of Mr. David Russell Hughes—his throat slit from ear to ear.

Chapter 2

Sunday, 5:30 a.m. Sugar Island Time

Hello. I'm trying to reach Mr. Jack Handler," a polite female voice said when Jack answered his phone.

"This is he. What can I do for you?" Jack said, squinting to focus his eyes on the face of his watch, which was lying on a nightstand beside his bed.

Five-thirty.

He turned onto his back and sucked in a large gulp of early-morning oxygen.

"Hope I didn't wake you, Mr. Handler, but Sheriff Green is eager to talk to you. Can you hold for a moment while I put him through?"

"Sure," Jack replied.

Holding his cell phone in his right hand, he first stretched both arms outward and then rubbed the night out of his eyes with his left hand. Placing the phone between his right ear and his pillow, he rolled his head onto it and stared straight ahead without focusing. He was trying to shake from his mind the last vestige of the blonde his dream had created.

He had been waiting over a week for the Sheriff to formally release Reginald Black's body for burial. So, despite it coming so early in the morning—and on a Sunday no less—he still did not mind the interruption.

Eight days earlier Sheriff Green had informed Jack that his detectives were prepared to sign off on the coroner's autopsy report—that Reginald Black had died from an accidental overdose of heroin.

Their decision was not easily reached, however. The obvious ligature marks on both wrists and ankles more than hinted that something more sinister was going on, but Jack convinced the sheriff that the smartest thing to do would be to accept the accidental aspect of the cause of death and allow justice to be served outside the courtroom.

Reg had been Jack's oldest and closest friend. While Jack knew that Reg had been the victim of a professional hit, and while he even knew who had contracted the murder, Jack was convinced that Chippewa County would never gain a conviction—not against Allison Fulbright, a former first lady.

For nearly two weeks, Jack petitioned the sheriff to pass on pushing the case through the Chippewa County court system. And finally it appeared the sheriff had become willing to take his advice. Without getting into too much detail, Jack had shared with the sheriff some of the convoluted circumstances that had occurred during the past year with regard to Reginald Black.

It was now more than a year ago that Reg had gone into hiding by faking his death. Reg was convinced at the time that he had no alternative. He had accepted one hundred million dollars in gold from Allison as payment for the assassination of Barry Butler, the sitting president.

Reg never wanted the job. In fact, he had been caught by surprise when Allison sought him out to head up the operation. So, hoping to dissuade Allison from going through with the plot, Reg set the price tag extraordinarily high.

But the price tag did not scare off Allison. Even though she was not happy with what Reg was seeking, Allison knew that he was the man best suited to carry out a job this important. So, she reluctantly accepted his price.

The plot that Reg and Allison devised was to blame the radical opposition for the assassination and then have the new president nominate her to serve out the remainder of his term as second in command.

At the end of the term, she intended to coerce the new president into refusing to run for a full term. She then would seek the nomination unopposed by her party—and practically unopposed in the general election. She calculated that the sympathy vote would not only sweep her into the Oval Office, but it would also provide the coattails to capture both the House and the Senate for her party.

However, Reg had a different plan—instead of actually carrying out the assassination, he hired Jack to work with him to thwart the plot.

And together they did just that.

With regard to the gold—even though Reg would happily have returned it to Allison, he knew that to do so would cost him his life. He simply knew too much for her to allow him to live.

Therefore, he thought it best to simply fake his death. And that's what he did.

With the help of one of Reg's and Jack's mutual friends, Secret Service Agent Roger Minsk, Reg had arranged to have his body declared dead. Roger, who just happened to head up Allison's Secret Service detail, set up the whole thing.

Reg, who had been grazed by a bullet in Brooklyn during a shootout with a group of rogue Eastern European agents (the same gunfight that saw Kate, Jack's daughter, struck in the kidney by a fragment of a stray bullet), was at first transported to the same hospital as was Kate to deal with his relatively minor wounds.

Most of the attention was paid to Kate's injuries, so no one noticed when Roger removed Reg from the hospital and transferred him to the care of a private physician.

As soon as he was able, Reg was then released from treatment, given a new identity, and relocated to Florida. And Reg Black was officially declared dead from heart failure.

Because Reg's death was deemed to be from "natural causes," no autopsy was ordered. Roger then arranged with Pam, Reg's "widow," for a closed-casket funeral at Calvary Cemetery in Queens, New York.

Jack and Pam even attended Reg's funeral together and were at the graveside when his coffin was lowered into the soil, yet neither of them were aware that it contained three burlap bags full of lake sand, but no body.

At the time, Allison was totally absorbed in avoiding the spotlight. Her assassination plot had just fallen apart, and she was busy trying to find refuge in the tall grass.

Later, however, once she had grown confident that she was going to be able to avoid public scrutiny regarding the failed plot, she started looking for her gold. She had decided to make another run for the White House, and she determined that the fortune she had turned over to Reg would be very helpful in her political pursuits.

However, the more she investigated, the greater her skepticism became regarding the circumstances surrounding Reg's death.

For one thing, she questioned why there had been no autopsy conducted on his body. Even though Reg's death had been documented as due to a heart attack—Allison knew that autopsies are generally done whenever there is a gunshot wound.

Once Allison had had a little time to scrutinize all the strange circumstances involved, she grew suspicious and began seeking to have Reg's body exhumed. While that effort was met with resistance from Pam Black, eventually her investigators made a startling discovery that was not directly associated with the alleged death of Reginald Black.

Earlier, Allison had carefully cataloged all the gold before she

turned it over to Reg. This list included the specific metal compo-
sition, sometimes referred to as a metal's "DNA," of nearly every
individual piece. She did this because most of the specimens were
uniquely identifiable works of art and, as such, would be very hard
to sell intact.

So, when gold bullion bearing the distinct characteristics of
some of the gold she had given to Reg began turning up in Miami,
she knew that someone, perhaps even Reg himself, was trying to
peddle it.

Once convinced she was on the right trail, she had her investigators buy the video of the person attempting to sell the gold. She
was not really surprised that the seller turned out to be a tall man
who, even though he was now sporting a full beard, bore an amazing resemblance to Reg.

It was at that point that she redoubled her efforts to have his
body exhumed. And when her efforts continued to be stubbornly
blocked by Reg's "widow," she simply dispatched a private investigator to monitor the Chippewa International Airport, knowing
that eventually Reg would attempt to confer with his good friend
Jack.

Allison's gamble paid off. Reg did fly into the UP to pay a surprise visit to Jack. Unfortunately, Reg spent less than one full day in
the Soo before he was found dead from an alleged heroin overdose.

Chapter 3

Sunday, 11:00 a.m. Sugar Island Time

Jack had been out of town when Reginald Black died. At first Sheriff Green had no clue that the body was that of one of Jack's close friends. Even after he was able, with the help of the FBI, to connect a name with the dead man's fingerprints through the IAFIS database, he still did not associate the name with Jack.

Not until he had talked to Jack regarding a different matter did he make the connection.

Jack told the sheriff that he had just learned that Reg was still alive and that he was caught entirely by surprise when had Reg called him the day before.

Once Jack made a positive identification of the body, the sheriff asked him what he thought about the ligature marks on the body. It appeared that someone had tightly secured Reg's wrists and ankles before he'd died.

Largely because of those ligature marks, it was the sheriff's initial theory that Reg had been murdered.

Knowing that nothing the sheriff could do would bring back his friend, Jack decided that it would be best for all concerned for the death to be declared accidental.

Jack explained to the sheriff that he had a pretty good notion as to who was ultimately responsible for Reg's murder, and that for the sheriff to pursue a criminal case against that person would be futile.

"Sheriff," Jack said, "If I'm right, and if the person I suspect for this crime is actually good for it, then this would be the quintessentially classic case of celebrity syndrome. There could be one hundred million eyewitnesses who saw this person shove the needle into Reg's arm, and if she denied committing the crime, she would be acquitted. That is, should the case ever even make it to trial.

"And if you actually did manage to make a strong case, you would most likely meet the same end as Reg did."

Sheriff Green knew Jack meant what he said, and so he reluctantly agreed to leave the whole matter in Jack's hands.

Little by little the constant barrage of complaints and petty incidents were turning Sheriff Green into a jaded member of the "good old boys club." He had basically inherited his position from a dirty cop, and he was finding that much of the stigma had carried over to him. He was beginning to find alcohol his preferred method of escaping his troubles. His hands were developing a bit of a tremor, and his constant flushed complexion bespoke the early signs of alcoholism. He was happy to give Jack the case to crack.

Jack had not yet determined how he would deal with Allison were it to turn out that she was the one responsible for Reg's death.

As far as he was concerned, Allison had a legitimate gripe against his friend. Reg had, after all, essentially stolen a fortune from her.

Not only that, but Jack was also troubled by the fact that, even though he had never received any compensation from Reg, he still had participated in the deception.

In Jack's mind, Reg had cheated at the high-stakes table and won. Notwithstanding the morality of his motivation, he still was a cheater who had gotten caught.

Jack was not yet certain exactly how he would react to the whole matter. Were he to know where the gold was hidden, he would most certainly see that it was returned to Allison.

But once it was returned, he had not yet determined what his next step would be.

And neither had Allison. She strongly suspected that were she to push the wrong buttons, Jack would exact revenge on her.

That's why she asked Roger to set up a meeting with Jack right after Reg's funeral. She wanted Roger to be present as well.

Her intention was to offer Jack a substantial finder's fee for the return of the gold. She was convinced that Reg had never paid

Jack, but she suspected that he might have shared with Jack some information that might be useful in finding the gold.

Initially, after discovering Reg was still alive, she suspected that he had hidden some or all of the gold in or below the grave where he was supposed to have been buried.

Once it was determined that Reg was not buried in Calvary Cemetery, Allison was able to bribe the gravediggers into exposing the coffin. When all that was found in the coffin were three bags of sand, and beneath the grave there also was no sign of the gold, she realized that the person most likely to be successful in finding the gold would be Jack.

And she also knew that if she were able to hire Jack, he would be relentless.

So, she was prepared to give him ten million dollars in cash up front. And then, if and when he found a substantial percentage of the gold, she would make a payment of ten percent of the value of that gold to Pam, Reg's widow.

She strongly suspected that Jack would accept the job—not on the basis of personal gain, but for Pam Black's sake. Allison knew that while the possibility of revenge was always there, Jack would still want to see the proper thing done.

And she was right.

When Roger told Jack that Allison wanted to meet with him, Jack asked his friend what she might be thinking. Roger, with Allison's permission, laid out the details to Jack about what she had in mind.

After only a few moments, Jack concluded that the offer was legitimate. He would be willing to give it his best shot.

His plan was to give the initial ten million dollars to Pam. And if he were able to find the gold, he would then deduct ten million dollars as a finder's fee—not exactly the same terms as Allison had in mind, but he knew she would find them acceptable.

Of course, once that transaction was complete, he could still consider killing Allison. He would just have to see how he felt about it at that time.

Chapter 4

Sunday, 11:30 a.m. Sugar Island Time

J ack. How the hell are you?"

"Sheriff. You got the news I've been waiting for?"

"Depends on what you're wanting to hear," the sheriff replied.

This guy is in some kind of good spirits, Jack thought. *Or has he been drinking?*

"Well," Jack said, "the funeral is scheduled for ten a.m. Wednesday. So, it would be nice if we could get a release on the body. ASAP."

"I'd say we're good to go on this," the sheriff said. "The prosecutor determined that while the autopsy did turn up some anomalies, such as the apparent ligature marks on his wrists and ankles, the actual cause of death remains an overdose of heroin, and that there is no compelling evidence to demonstrate that it was *not* self-administered. So, the official cause of death remains as originally thought—an accidental drug overdose.

"That having been said, you may officially take possession of Reginald Black's remains any time after Monday morning at ten a.m."

"Okay, sheriff," Jack said. "I appreciate your effort on my behalf. I promise you that this is the right decision, for everyone concerned."

"When are you leaving?"

"My flight is scheduled for one-forty on Tuesday," Jack said. "By the way, what are you doing in your office on a Sunday? And this early in the morning? What time is it, anyway?"

"I'm not actually in my office," the sheriff said. "I'm down in lockup. I had a call early this morning that we might have a potential witness in this Reginald Black business. Someone who was seen coming out of Mr. Black's room shortly before the 911 call. I thought I should question him before I released the body, just in case."

"And what did the witness have to say?" Jack asked.

"Not much, actually," the sheriff said. "When I got here I found the potential witness with his throat cut."

"In a holding cell?"

"Not exactly," the sheriff said. "He was all by himself in an interrogation room. Strange. Right?"

"Yeah," Jack replied. "Strange. So, you'll have all the necessary paperwork ready for me in time for my Tuesday flight?"

"How do you plan to handle it?" the sheriff asked.

"I would like to have Griffon's, the funeral home, take care of it. I've chosen a coffin for Reg. They'll pick up the body as soon as possible and then deliver it in time to catch the one-forty flight. I'll coordinate it with them—the terminal, time, and the airline. We should be good as long as the body gets released to them okay."

"I'll take care of it," the sheriff said.

"Got anybody in mind for slicing up your prisoner?" Jack asked.

The sheriff did not want to discuss it. "You just please get this Reg guy, your buddy, out of my county and back in the ground— this time for good. Will you just do that for me? And maybe you should consider just staying in New York."

"Can't do that, sheriff," Jack replied. "For one thing, you'd miss me too much. And for a second thing, if I moved back to Chicago *or* New York, who'd run this resort? Sugar Island would miss me."

"Jack," the sheriff said. "Trust me, no one in the state of Michigan would ever miss you. You are nothing but trouble."

"I love you too, sheriff. And thanks for your help with Reg's body. I owe you one."

"You owe me a whole hell of a lot more than that," Sheriff Green replied. "But I'd consider the debt paid in full if you just never came back. If you left the UP, moved in with your daughter in New York ... and just stayed there. Think about it, Jack. Nothing would make me happier."

"Sheriff Green. I know that secretly you are in love with me. You just have a hard time expressing your real feelings."

The sheriff flashed a sincere smile, of which only he was aware, and then he said, "Give my best to Kate, and remember to duck. On second thought—*don't* duck!"

"Thanks for the advice, sheriff," Jack said. "And, seriously, what have you got on your prisoner? Who killed him?"

"Suicide," the sheriff said.

"Right."

"I'm serious. It had to have been suicide," the sheriff said. "There was no one in the room with him."

"And how did he manage that?"

"Apparently he had a razor blade taped to the side of his face. When we locked him in the interrogation room, he removed it and slit his own throat. We found pieces of the razor blade in his mouth. He'd chewed it up and tried to swallow it before he died.

"Look, Handler, just do this county a favor and take your buddy back to New York. And this time bury him so he *stays* buried."

Chapter 5

Sunday, 12:30 p.m. in Paris

Who is this guy? I thought. *He's* way *too friendly.*

Jill and I were attending an international Mass at Notre Dame. We had stood in a cold, rainy line for nearly half an hour, waiting for those who had attended the earlier Mass to leave the cathedral. I was happy to finally be inside and seated.

But as for the tall fellow sitting beside Jill—I did not appreciate his aggressive familiarity.

It was bad enough that I could understand virtually nothing that was said by the priest, but because we had entered so late, our seats were behind one of the huge limestone pillars that supported the roof of the magnificent structure. Only a few times was I able to catch even a brief glimpse of the proceedings in the Gregorian Mass—except, of course, what was going on to my left.

Initially, I dismissed their chatter to Jill's simply trying to be friendly. She had a particularly disarming way of winning over people she had just met. Her appealing smile, bright blue eyes, and long blonde hair, which today she wore tied back with a ribbon, made her irresistible. When conversing with friends or strangers, Jill could always make them sense her genuine interest in what they were saying.

Tiny by any standard, today she appeared exceptionally so as she looked up into the face of this very tall man.

He did speak English, so that made communication easy. Over the course of our stay in Paris, we seldom met English speakers, aside from those asking directions or trying to scam us.

But when Jill pulled her digital camera out of her black zipper bag and began to show him some of the pictures she had taken, I started to question the appropriateness of their conversation. We were, after all, in the middle of a "solemn Mass" according to the bulletin handed to us upon our being seated.

And then she activated her smartphone, logged onto her Web page, and began scrolling through some of the fine art photos she displayed there. He was impressed. Twice he pointed to a piece of art with his pinky finger, and at least once he grabbed her hand as they viewed the various pieces, ostensibly to have her describe a particular image. They kept their voices low, so I could not understand what exactly they were saying.

Finally, Jill put her phone back into her bag and then removed a business card and handed it to the man. He subsequently scribbled something on the back of his card and handed it to her. When she read what he had written, she smiled, said something to him, and placed it in her bag.

I'll admit that I was very interested in what they had discussed, and even more in what prompted the exchange of cards. At that time, it would not have been correct to regard my emotion as jealousy. But, eventually I did question the events of that afternoon, not the least of which was the nature of her conversation with that tall stranger.

Chapter 6

Sunday, 12:38 p.m. in Paris

A fter a bit, everything settled down, and both Jill and I returned to our pointless attempt to appreciate the chants. And, at first, the man seated beside Jill seemed to do the same.

His three boys, however, had become thoroughly bored. Suddenly, the oldest stood up and tore off toward the western end of the cathedral. Just before he jumped from his seat, I had caught out of the corner of my eye one of his younger siblings finger-flicking his ear lobe.

The tall man turned in his seat, trying to determine exactly where his son was headed and to figure out what the boy might have in mind. At first he seemed content to allow his son to burn off some energy. But then, probably realizing that the boy appeared about to leave Notre Dame, he excused himself to Jill, took his other two sons, and followed after.

I thought the matter was resolved until the oldest boy returned to where we were sitting. He had circled back and was now looking for his father.

Jill spoke briefly to him and then rose from her seat, at the same time snatching the black zipper bag.

"I'll be back," she said, "I'm gonna help him find his father."

For a moment, I thought of going with her. But she hurried off so quickly I would not have had time to gather up our camera equipment and our umbrella. I did turn to follow her with my eyes as her red North Face parka, with her long blonde hair bouncing on its hood, disappeared into the crowd with the boy in tow.

Chapter 7

Sunday, 12:55 p.m. in Paris

I sat for the next fifteen minutes, growing more and more concerned. Everyone in the congregation then stood. I surmised that the priest had directed us to greet one another. A balding middle-aged man who sat in front of us to the left shook hands with an elderly lady to his right, saying something to her in French.

He then turned and, with a smile, extended his hand to me. The man directly to my right did the same. The woman, however—while she turned, smiled, and nodded her head in a friendly fashion—did not extend her hand to me. A lavender shawl, which she wore over her head, allowed a few small strands of gray to escape on each side, forming a tight frame around her small, round face. She had to have been less than five feet tall and weighed ninety pounds at most. She struck me as a local resident who attended regularly. I assumed her tiny hands, gnarled from long-untreated arthritis, probably did not handle well that international gesture of greeting.

I surmised that she knew the man to her left—they probably sat together every Sunday. One thing about the French, at least the ones I met, when they shake hands they do so in a soft fashion—as though they were cautiously placing a warm, damp cloth in your hand.

She probably knew it was safe to shake hands with him. But, having overheard me speaking English, correctly surmised that I was an American and feared that to shake hands with me could cause her pain.

Chapter 8

Sunday, 1:10 p.m. in Paris

For just a moment, the meet-and-greet distracted me. When I looked at my watch again, it was one-ten—Jill had been gone nearly twenty minutes. That was much longer than I had anticipated.

I picked up my camera and umbrella, stood, and slid over to

the end of the row where they had been seated. There I would not be so much of a distraction. Slowly I scoured the main sanctuary, like the captain of a submarine might survey the horizon through his periscope—particularly in the direction of their disappearance. But I could not find Jill or the boy.

Jill and I had discussed earlier what to do in the event that we were ever to get separated in an unfamiliar city. We decided that if and when that should happen, as soon as it was clear to one of us, that we would immediately stop, try to make ourselves as visible as possible, and wait. Even though my instincts told me that I should go after her, I stuck with the game plan.

But the longer I waited, the more anxious I became.

What if this turned out to be some sort of abduction? I asked myself. Scenes from the movie *Taken* flashed through my mind.

"That's crazy," I concluded. That's when a whole battery of ugly thoughts began to rush through my mind.

What if she had suffered a heart attack? As far as I knew she was in good health. But the change of sleeping patterns and diet—perhaps they suddenly got the better of her, and she fainted. Or maybe became disoriented.

What if a blood clot formed on the eight-hour flight from the US? I've heard of that happening. And maybe it made its way to her heart or her brain.

All sorts of random thoughts raced through my mind.

I wonder what was in the note that man handed her, I said to myself. Could it be he had something sinister in mind? It was not exactly like he was flirting with her, but it was not far from it. And she did seem to like whatever he was saying. At least that is how it appeared.

I still remained standing at the end of my row. I looked around at the people seated nearby, and it did not seem as though I was a distraction. So I continued to do my best to find her blonde hair somewhere in the crowd.

Chapter 9

Sunday, 1:15 p.m. in Paris

B y this time, I estimated that twenty-five minutes had passed. My concern was turning into panic. Soon the Mass would be finished, and everyone would stand. That would make it much more difficult for me to find her. I considered leaving my post but then recalled that we were firm in our resolve as to how to handle matters such as this. If we ever got separated, the one left behind would wait to be found—no time limit. And I was the one left behind.

Clearly, when she initially rose from her seat, she told me that she would be "right back." That established firmly that she intended to return to where she had left me. Given our earlier plan of action, I had no choice but to wait.

Chapter 10

Sunday, 1:20 p.m. in Paris

Even though I did not understand what the priest had said, I knew what was happening. The congregation stood and began filing toward the front for communion. I checked my watch. It was now a half hour since she had left. Nothing should have taken her that long—at least nothing that I could think of.

After another ten minutes, I concluded that something very unusual was taking place. I began to design an alternate plan of action.

I turned and walked toward the main exit—that was the last place I had seen Jill.

It took several minutes to reach the doors because the whole congregation was beginning to make its way there as well.

As I moved through the crowd, I elevated my sight as high as I could, trying to peer over the tops of people's heads. Still I did not spot her.

Just before I reached the door, I stepped aside and again looked out over the crowd toward the front of the cathedral—especially in the direction of where we had been seated.

If she had returned from a different direction, I reasoned, *she would have gone back to where she left me and be waiting there.*

Chapter 11

Sunday, 1:35 p.m. in Paris

After searching from a distance the whole area where we had been seated, but not seeing Jill, I again checked my watch.

"Forty-four minutes," I mumbled.

I then allowed my eyes to take another panoramic examination of the awe-inspiring cathedral and the twelve to fifteen hundred people contained within it.

Most of them are praying, I thought. *Perhaps that's what I should have done.*

It was very difficult for me to bring myself to the point of leaving Notre Dame—I thought it a little like surrendering territory to a foreign adversary. But it now felt like the logical thing to do. After all, the last time I had seen Jill she was walking in the direction of the exit. It seemed right.

Damn, I thought. We had talked about packing a set of two-way radios but had forgotten them. Or, perhaps we simply didn't think they would be that useful.

As we had done on previous visits to Paris, we activated only one cell phone. We had intended to stay close together, so two phones should not have been necessary. Besides, we were trying to cut expenses.

We just never envisioned this type of scenario.

I knew that once I walked out the door, getting back in would be a bit of a challenge. I got in the exit line and eventually filed outside.

My eyes immediately found the waiting line for the next Mass. It extended more than two hundred feet into the plaza, well up the steps of the temporary structure constructed as a viewing area for the opening ceremonies celebrating Notre Dame's eight hundred and fiftieth anniversary.

If Jill had left the cathedral with the boy, most likely she would have been forced to get back in the line in order to re-enter, I reasoned. So I hurried up the line all the way to the end, carefully searching for Jill, the tall man, or any of his sons. They were not there.

It was raining harder than before, but I didn't engage my umbrella. I thought it might obstruct my vision.

Once thoroughly satisfied that neither Jill nor our recent encounters were waiting to re-enter, I determined that if Jill had decided to search outside for me, she would most likely be doing so directly in front of the cathedral. And my best view of that area would be from the top of the observation platform. From there I could see not only the entire façade of Notre Dame, but also the bridge across the Seine Jill would take should she for some strange reason decide to return to our hotel.

Once positioned atop the northwest corner of the viewing area, I began scrutinizing the people moving below.

Drops of rain had totally flattened my hair and had begun dripping off my chin. Finally, I succumbed to using the umbrella.

I felt chilled. My body reacted by shaking. While it was tolerably chilly—three degrees centigrade that morning—the rain and a steady breeze off the Seine made it very uncomfortable. The fact that my emotions were out of control certainly contributed to my discomfort, as did the water that had totally soaked my leather jacket.

Suddenly I felt an uncontrollable urge to urinate. I knew that I needed to deal with it promptly. A huge line made it impossible for me to get back into Notre Dame quickly enough, so I ran down the steps as rapidly as I could.

At first I headed toward the river. But I spotted dozens of tourists walking to and from that area, even in the rain. I decided I would do better to find a side street just off the main complex. I opted for Pont d'Arcole. Street vendors occupied the sidewalk that ran parallel to the cathedral on the north; however, none were set up on this side street.

It is common practice for men to openly relieve themselves in

Paris. While I had done this before, it was always at night when children were scarce. Under normal conditions, I would not have even considered urinating in the vicinity of the austere edifice of Notre Dame. But today I had no choice.

As I darted down Pont d'Arcole, looking for any inset doorway, I was not concerned with adults observing me from behind, but I did not want children around. I reasoned the worst that could happen would be for law enforcement to take me into custody. Were that to happen, I then might be able to engage their help in finding Jill.

I squeezed into the first doorway that seemed to provide acceptable cover and relieved myself.

Chapter 12

Sunday, 1:50 p.m. in Paris

O n my way back to my lookout post, I checked my watch. "One hour exactly," I muttered. Hurriedly I pushed my way to the top of the stairs, two and three steps at a time, and there resumed my lookout.

This was beginning to feel futile. But what else could I do? I started considering alternatives.

The police, I thought. *It's been an hour. I must engage the police.*

I had earlier observed that there were two groups of law enforcement in Paris. Some wore camo and carried automatic weapons—those I suspected were French military. They generally were on the move, patrolling in groups of three. I was looking for those wearing the navy blue uniforms and black boots—the Police Nationale.

Thankfully, there is always a healthy contingent of blue uniforms around Notre Dame. I looked for a group of officers. My reasoning—I would stand a better chance of finding an English-speaking officer were I to seek out a gathering of three or four.

I quickly spotted several officers standing together at the north end of the Pont au Double bridge, just south of the plaza.

Once close enough to be heard, I said loudly, "English. Does anyone speak English? I have an emergency."

They looked at one another, as though deciding who should deal with this mouthy American.

The tallest of the three turned and looked me directly in the eye and cleared his throat: "Monsieur, what's the problem?"

Whether real or affected, I thought I detected a note of concern in his voice.

However, the other two officers each took one step backward and placed a hand on their batons. That told me I needed to exercise caution.

I knew that if I simply reported that my fiancée was lost or missing, I would not get their attention.

"My fiancée's been kidnapped! Abducted!"

"Really? What makes you think that?"

I sensed his concern had morphed into skepticism. I knew I

had to be convincing.

"She was abducted by a large man … very tall … from *inside* Notre Dame."

"You saw this?"

"Yes," I replied as compellingly as possible.

My thinking was that it would be better to have them looking for two people, rather than just my fiancée. If they were to locate the man, he might be able to guide them to Jill.

The officer to whom I was talking turned to one of the other officers and gave him a command in French. I assume it was for backup or a car, as the second officer immediately pulled out his radio and keyed it.

He then turned to me and asked, "What is your name?"

"Paul, my name is Paul Martin."

"And your fiancée, what is her name?"

"Jill Talbot."

"Okay. Thank you, Monsieur Martin. How would you describe your fiancée, and the man you say abducted her? What do they look like? What were they wearing? Do you know his name—"

"I do *not* know the man's name," I interrupted. "My fiancée is five feet, six inches. Blonde. Thin. Pretty. Twenty-two years old. She was wearing a red North Face parka—that's a type of coat, with a hood. She had matching rain boots—they matched her coat. But she wasn't wearing the hood up. Instead, she wore a black hat. That is, when she went outside. And she had a black zippered bag. Not a purse. It was a cloth bag. Probably nylon."

"Then your fiancée was much younger than you? Is that not correct? And exactly how old are you, Monsieur Martin?"

"I am a *little* older. I'm thirty."

"I see," the officer said, looking over at his partner for a moment. And then he continued, "And the kidnapper—what did he look like?"

But before I could respond, an angry man approached us from behind.

"That's him!" he shouted in American English, sticking his finger in my nose as I turned to face him.

"He was just pissing in the street," he said. "Right in front of my children."

"Over there," he continued, his voice rising as he pointed to where I had just been.

"Do you know what he's talking about?" the officer asked, peering into my eyes.

"I had to take a leak, so went across the street, where he pointed, and urinated in a doorway. But there were no children within a hundred feet. No one saw anything except my back."

"Have you been drinking?" he asked me.

"No, my fiancée and I had just attended Mass. That's where the tall man kidnapped her. I came outside and looked around for some police. I was nervous. The rain made me cold. And I have a weak bladder. I did what I had to do—I walked over there, where no one could see, and I took a leak."

My explanation was obviously good enough because the officer thanked and excused my accuser: "Thank you, sir. We've got him now. I'll take care of it. Thank you very much."

He then turned back to me: "Now, tell me about this man. What did he look like? What was he wearing? Did he have a weapon? What exactly makes you think he kidnapped your fiancée … and that she didn't just go with him because she wanted to?"

Chapter 13

Sunday, 2:00 p.m. in Paris

A t that time, two police cars pulled up, and the officer who was questioning me grabbed my arm and pushed me into the back seat of one of them. He then motioned that I slide to the other side, and he slipped in beside me. He ceased talking to me for a while and instead conversed in French with the two officers in the front seat.

After a few moments, he turned back to me and asked, "Monsieur, please help me understand this. Are you saying that some man abducted your fiancée from inside Notre Dame?"

"Yes. Exactly."

"From inside? And you did not protest? And no one in the cathedral tried to stop him?"

"That's right. It was during Mass."

"How did he manage to do that, this mystery man? Did he threaten you? Did he show you a weapon? Did your girlfriend scream? Or put up a struggle?"

It was becoming clear to me that the abduction angle might not be working, but I still considered it my best hope.

"We were at Mass. This tall man walked in after we did and sat down beside my fiancée. They talked for a bit, and he handed her a note, which she read and placed in her bag. After about ten minutes, his children began fighting with each other. And one, the oldest boy, took off in a fit of temper. It looked like he was headed toward the exit. When the tall man lost sight of his son, he gathered up his other two children and went off after the angry son."

"At this time your fiancée is still at Mass, and the man was gone? Did he then return? To abduct your fiancée?"

"No, but the first son did—the one who had run off."

"How old was this boy? Was he the actual kidnapper? The boy?"

I could see by their smirks that all three officers doubted my story.

"Certainly not, but I imagine he could have been in on it. He seemed to be looking for his father. He was crying. My fiancée then excused herself, took the boy, and disappeared in the direction that the father had gone. That was the last I saw of her."

All three officers talked among themselves in French. Finally, the one seated beside me asked, "Had you been fighting? You and your girlfriend?"

"No. Absolutely not. We've not even spoken a cross word since we've been in Paris."

"And how long has that been? When did you arrive?"

"Two days. We actually arrived yesterday."

For a long uncomfortable moment, the officer seated next to me silently stared into the eyes of the driver, who had intentionally adjusted the mirror for that purpose. It was as though they each could read the other's mind. And then he raised his eyebrows and turned back toward me. "Okay, sir, I'm going to need some more information from you."

His tone now was one of total disbelief. And the questions he asked had nothing to do with any effort directed at finding the man whom I suspected of kidnapping Jill. At least that's how it seemed to me. He gathered information about Jill and me—where we were from, our hotel in Paris, how long we planned to stay, if Jill had her passport with her. And then he asked again if we had been arguing.

He needed some information for his report. And that's what he was gathering—information for a potential missing person report—not a kidnapping.

Finally, he took a business card out of his wallet.

"Monsieur Martin," he said. "This is my name—Claude Henreid. And this is the number you can use to call me. For right now we are going to wait and see if your girlfriend comes back. Let me know when she does. But, if she does not, after three days, call me anyway."

"Then, you're not going to look for her for a few days? You've not even taken any information about her kidnapper. You're not going to be looking for him? Is that right?"

The three police officers looked at each other again, and the driver gestured with his hand to the officer doing the interview.

"Yes, tell me about that man—what he looked like, his age, how he was dressed, and the approximate ages of his children."

"He was tall. Well-dressed—a dark sports jacket over a sweater. He had a black raincoat. I would guess him to be in his early-to-mid-forties. Short dark hair, possibly a hat. I don't remember. Yes, he did have a hat. I remember him putting it on as he stood up to leave. It made him look even taller. And I thought it a little strange, that he'd wear a hat inside the cathedral."

"He was a handsome man? Would you describe him as a good-looking man? Was he trim, or would you say he was heavy?"

"He looked fit. I noticed he had very nice teeth."

I then observed that the three officers again exchanged a knowing glance.

"He was a trim, good-looking man, well dressed … and he had *three* sons? Could you describe his children?"

"I would estimate that they ranged in age from six to twelve. Like I said—it was the oldest one who left with my fiancée."

"Okay, Mr. Martin, we're going to file this report. We'll check the hospitals. Oh, do you have a picture of your girlfriend?"

"No," I said, "not with me."

And then I thought for a moment: "Her passport. I have her passport in the safe at the hotel. You can come over and take a look."

Chapter 14

Sunday, 2:30 p.m. in Paris

No, not right now. But if she is still missing in three days, call me, or come down to our office. The Police Nationale—the address is on the card I gave you. Actually, it's right over there," he said, pivoting to point in the general direction of a large building just west of the plaza. "The office is right over there—it's easy to find. Bring your fiancée's passport and yours. I will then introduce you to an investigator, and he will take it from there. That is, if you don't see her in the next three days."

"Then you're not going to look for her now?"

"Monsieur Martin, my hands are tied. There is not enough evidence for an investigation of an abduction. Your fiancée walked off of her own free will. We can't even proceed on it as a missing person. Not until it is established as such. And I can't make that determination on the basis of the information you've provided.

"But I will file a report, and if anything comes up regarding it, if we get anything on a Jill Talbot, we will contact you. That is the best we can do for right now. I'm truly sorry. I know you are concerned. But there just isn't enough evidence for me to give to an investigator. Please give me a call when you hear from her. Believe me, I am *very* concerned."

"This stinks! That's all I can say. My fiancée is in *serious* trouble, and you're not going to do a damn thing!"

"Like I said, my hands are tied. I can drop you off at your hotel if you'd like."

"No, I'm going to keep looking. I'm going to do *your* job."

I was very angry. As I started to get out of the car, the officer said, "Bonjour, Monsieur Martin. I truly am sorry. Please call me when you see her."

I know I was rude, but I just jumped out of the car and slammed the door.

At least I got warm, I thought. *And they did take a report. Her name is now on file, so if something comes up, maybe they will call me. Maybe.*

I continued walking around Notre Dame, inside and out, for over two hours. I searched for the tall man and his sons as much as for Jill—but without success.

The rain finally stopped.

I decided to go back to the hotel. Because I had no cell phone, if the police wanted to reach me they would have to do it through the hotel. I needed to give the desk clerk a heads-up.

Chapter 15

Sunday, 4:55 p.m. in Paris

The walk back usually took us about twelve minutes, but this time I made it in seven.

"Bonjour," I said to Claire.

I was happy to see that she was on duty. In her youth, Claire had studied in New York. She lived in White Plains for a couple years, so she knew English very well. I praised her English diction and teased her that she spoke my language better than I.

She was a petite girl in her twenties, with dark brown, very short hair and a nice smile. It was always a little awkward for me when she smiled because her teeth were unusually crooked.

As is common with many young Parisian women, she dressed mostly in black sweaters, black pencil skirts, and black boots. Her eyes were brown and heavily made up. And she was fond of bright scarves—usually red or yellow.

"Bonjour, Monsieur," Claire replied with her typical warm smile.

"Have you seen my fiancée?" I asked.

A look of concern immediately gripped her face. She knew that something up.

"No, I have not seen her. What's wrong?"

"She disappeared from Notre Dame. We were at Mass. I thought she might have returned to the hotel."

"Oh, no! What happened?"

I could tell by her undivided attention to me that she was genuinely concerned. Another guest arrived, and she handed him his key without taking her eyes off mine. The phone rang, and she let it go to voicemail.

"I don't know. She just simply tried to help this boy. She walked out of Mass. And that's the last I saw her. That was about five hours ago. If the police find her, they might call the hotel. Could you make sure the other people who work the desk know about this?"

"*Oui*, Monsieur. I'm so sorry."

"I don't have a cell phone, so I'm going to check in with the front desk frequently and ask for any messages."

"She walked off during Mass? How very strange."

"I know. The police suspect that we had an argument and that she left with the man."

"A man?"

"Yes. The boy's father. My fiancée was trying to help the boy find his father. We had met the man earlier."

"Oh, that is terrible."

"I'm going to get some dry clothes on and go back out. You'll make sure everyone knows to leave me a message? And that the police might be calling?"

"Oui, Monsieur. I'll write a note for the others." And then she said again, "I am so very sorry."

"Thanks," I said, taking my key from Claire and heading for the elevator.

Claire was wonderful. She had done everything she could to make our visit pleasant. When we checked in she upgraded our reservation from a double room to a triple—at no extra cost. Because we were staying for several days, she thought we should have a larger space.

Hotel rooms in Paris are small—and especially so in the Latin Quarter. A triple room was about nine feet longer than a double.

I had earlier calculated that our triple room was about nine feet wide and fourteen feet long. Add about four feet at the end for a small hall and closet and another five feet for the bath. That meant that the entire living space was probably around twenty-three by nine, while the standard double room measured about fourteen by nine.

Even the larger room did not provide much space to move around in, but still not bad by Latin Quarter standards.

So, here I was—cold and wet in a small Paris hotel, without any notion as to where Jill was.

I was terrified. I felt like breaking down and crying. But I stopped myself.

"What *can* I do?" I repeatedly asked myself.

The police had requested a picture. I could print one. I had images of her on my MacBook, and I always packed a lightweight HP color printer when we traveled. I could make up a "missing person" flier and take it to the police station. And I could show one around Notre Dame. If I hurried, I might even catch some of the tourists who were there when she'd disappeared.

I ran back downstairs.

"Claire. How do I write this in French? 'Have you seen this person?'

"I'm going to make up some sheets and post them in the area. I'll put my name and the hotel's phone number on it."

She knew exactly what I wanted. Directly under what I had written, she wrote, "*Est-ce que tu l'as vu?*" She then slid the paper back to me and smiled.

"I think that would be okay," she said.

"Do I have the hotel phone number correct?"

"Oui. That's correct."

"Thanks," I said, as I hurried back toward the elevator.

I resized, copied, and pasted an image of Jill onto a Word doc and typed above the picture "Est-ce que tu l'as vu?"

Beneath that I typed in English, "Jill Talbot. Have you seen this woman?"

At the bottom, I put the hotel's phone number. I thought that was clear enough.

I had only ten pieces of paper left, so I printed eight. I could always make more, but that would do the job for now.

Chapter 16

Sunday, 5:20 p.m. in Paris

I hurried back downstairs and left one of the sheets with Claire. She looked approvingly and taped it to the top of the front desk.

I figured my first stop should be the police station.

I changed my mind on the way. Instead, I headed back to where I had first encountered Officer Claude. He might still be on duty, I reasoned. Besides, I needed to apologize for my bad attitude.

It took me only a few short moments to locate him. In fact, he found me first.

Chapter 17

Sunday, 5:30 p.m. in Paris

B onsoir, Monsieur," he said as he approached me.

"Officer Henreid," I said. "I want to apologize for my attitude before. I understand your position. I am sorry."

"I can appreciate your frustration," he replied. "Have you heard from your fiancée yet?"

"No, but I do have a picture," I said, handing one of the sheets to him. "Do you think this might help?"

"Oui. Oui," he said, taking the flier and studying it. "She is very beautiful. I will include this with the report. *Merci beaucoup*."

In the US, his comment about Jill would be considered inappropriate. But in Paris, it's only polite for a man to notice a beautiful woman. I was not offended. In fact, by the way he looked at me I sensed for the first time the incident was being taken seriously.

Could it be, I wondered, that he now might be suspecting that perhaps I'd concocted this whole story as a cover-up? And that just maybe I had caused Jill's disappearance?

Officer Henreid was not an investigator, but he was no Inspector Clouseau either. Claude Henreid was a dignified "Police Nationale," a seasoned cop—or "flic," as cops are called in Paris. I'm sure that he had seen many more cases of domestic violence than he had kidnappings. And the longer this case remained unresolved, the more the police would regard me as a suspect, perhaps even as a potential *killer*.

All these thoughts raced through my head before I responded to him. I even concluded that this could work to my advantage. If he began to suspect me he would be more inclined to move the matter to the next level and engage an investigator. It could make life hell for me, but right now nothing was going to get done on their end.

"And she's still missing. I'm going to post some of these around Notre Dame …"

"No, no, no, Monsieur," he said, shaking his finger in my face. "Not permitted."

"Well, then you just might have to arrest me. You know where I'm staying. And the phone number is right here on the bottom."

"I'm serious, Monsieur Martin. You can't do that. It is against the law."

"I understand. Have you heard anything about my fiancée?"

"Not yet. But this picture will help."

"I'll call you tomorrow," I said as I walked away. "Thank you."

"*Au revoir*, Monsieur. And remember what I said, it is strictly against the law to post these around Notre Dame," Officer Henreid said, holding up the flier.

"Au revoir," I responded, smiling as I prepared to depart.

I turned and walked directly toward the cathedral. I wanted him to know that I was going to do exactly as I had threatened, even though it could result in my arrest. He did not come after me. And I did post all but one of the remaining notices—most of them across the street from Notre Dame but a couple in the plaza itself.

For the next two hours, I pushed the last poster in as many faces as possible and asked in English if they had seen this woman. Most did not understand what I said, but I think they still got the idea. Sadly, no one responded in the affirmative.

Chapter 18

Sunday, 7:30 p.m. in Paris

It had begun raining again, causing the picture of Jill to significantly degrade. I wadded it up and tossed it in a receptacle.

There was no point in continuing. I decided to go back to the hotel, ask them for some printer paper, and start over.

The trip from the cathedral to the hotel took longer than usual this time, but not because I was giving up the fight. I simply did not know what I should do, and so I took my time and thought heavily about how to proceed.

When I reached the hotel, I was happy to see that Claire was still working. I asked her for some printer paper and something to put over one to protect it from the rain.

She immediately gave me nearly half a ream and a clear plastic sleeve.

"Will this work?" she asked.

"Perfectly," I replied. "Thank you very much."

She did not respond.

"Have there been any messages for me?" I asked.

"No, Monsieur, I'm sorry," she said, handing me my key.

"Thank you," I said, turning toward the elevator.

Just before I stepped into the elevator, I realized that the poster of Jill was no longer taped to the desk.

"You removed the picture of Jill?" I asked.

"Sorry, Monsieur. The manager came in and told me I could not leave it there. It was against hotel policy. But I will make sure to keep asking other guests. I have it right here."

She then held up the poster. The corners were ripped off where the tape had secured it to the desk. I thought it looked like the manager, probably under protest by Claire, had tersely torn it off the desk.

I entered my room and immediately turned to my computer. After I had printed twenty-five copies, I slid one into the plastic cover Claire had given me and headed back to Notre Dame. This time I took my umbrella. Even though the picture of Jill was more protected than before, still it would not stand up under the heavy rain that was again beginning to fall.

I have always had an aversion to wearing hats, but I needed something to keep the chill from creeping back into my body. So I gave eight euros to a street vendor and bought a plain black cap with a visor. As soon as I pulled it over my wet head, I began to feel a little better.

Chapter 19

Sunday,
10:00 p.m. in Paris

Walking through the streets well into the night, I pushed the picture of Jill in front of every person I possibly could. Surprisingly, I did not receive a single angry response. In every case, the answer was "no," but no one seemed offended.

In the cases of those who spoke English, they would express concern and encouragement. Many told me they would pray for Jill.

By ten-thirty I was exhausted. And the crowd had largely disappeared. Now about the only people hanging around in the plaza were either drunk or seeking that escape. I decided to go back to the hotel. I needed to let our families know that something had gone terribly wrong.

I sent the same email to all of her sisters and something similar to my brother. It read like this:

"This has been a horrible day. Your sister has disappeared. We were in Notre Dame for Mass this morning, and she left with a young boy who had lost his father. She was trying to help him. She did not come back. I have contacted the police, and they are looking for her. I made up posters and placed them around Notre Dame. I then spent the rest of the day and evening asking people around the cathedral if they had seen her. I got no positive response. Tomorrow I will go back to the police station and see if they've heard anything. I know that this must make you feel helpless. I feel the same way. I also know that I have let you down by not protecting her. I can do nothing about that now, except to keep looking. I will email you as often as I can to bring you up to date. If any of you hear from her, let me know immediately via email. You can also call the hotel and they can ring my room. It's eleven here right now, so that makes it five in the evening for you. I know you won't sleep tonight. I'm sorry to do this to you, but I felt you should know what's going on.

"For now, please keep this to yourselves. At least use discretion. You might not want to tell your father, as he is frail. But you guys must make that call. Chances are it will all turn out just fine, so you might not want to worry him unnecessarily. Again, the best way to contact me is email or by calling the hotel. Your sister has our cell phone. –Paul."

Within minutes, I heard from all three of Jill's siblings. The questions were all the same: "How could this happen? Have you heard anything? What can we do from here? Should we get our passports renewed?"

Only one of them, Jill's older sister Lesley, had a valid passport. She immediately wanted to get her ticket to come to Paris. I suggested she hold off at least for a couple days. Perhaps we would hear something by then. I felt that I should have a clearer head by morning and that I would keep contacting them.

My brother was devastated. He offered to come over as well, but I strongly discouraged his doing so.

I spent the next several hours fielding emailed questions from her family, such as "have you tried to call her cell?"

To which I replied that her cell was not being answered.

But I heard nothing from the police.

I could not sleep. I played white noise on my computer all night but to no avail.

Chapter 20

Monday, 9:00 a.m. in Paris

Finally, around nine in the morning, the phone in my room rang. I must have drifted off, so the ringing of the phone nearly shattered my head.

"Hello," I said, after fumbling for the phone.

"Monsieur Martin. This is the front desk. We have two Police Nationale here, and they want to talk to you."

"Okay. I'll be right down."

"You won't have to come down. They are on their way up."

Well, they were not only "on their way up." By the time I hung up the phone the police were already pounding on my door.

"Monsieur Martin," the one speaking English said. "We're from the Police Nationale. Please open the door."

And then he knocked again, only louder.

"Open the door, please!"

I was nearly in shock. I don't remember exactly what they said after that, only that they made it clear I needed to go with them for questioning.

Insisting that I leave the bathroom door open, they did allow me a few minutes to get dressed but not to shave or shower. I took my dry jeans and black shirt into the bathroom and quickly changed, slipped on my boots and headed back down the stairs to the street. They put me into the back of the police car, and we headed to the station. No one was smiling.

The next three hours seemed more like five. And they were hell. While there were always two and sometimes three police officers in the small room with me, only one spoke. He identified himself as an "investigator with Police Nationale." He told me his last name but I didn't understand him. He also gave me his card. But, even with it, I still could not pronounce his last name, so I simply addressed him by his first: "Investigator Pierre."

His English was polished—I suspect he had spent years in the US. He had all the idioms perfect.

I was pleased that my situation was now being taken seriously, but I was not happy with the tone or direction of the inquisition.

"Oh, and by the way, Monsieur Martin. We are searching your room right now. I hope that is okay with you."

Even though nothing had been suggested to that point that our room would be searched, I had assumed that it would be.

"That's fine," I replied. The investigator studied my response. "Do whatever is necessary to find my fiancée.

"But you'll not discover anything there that will help you find her. Neither of us had any notion our trip would turn out like this. It just happened. And you would do well to track down that man … the tall man … and his three sons. They were the last ones to see her."

"What do you mean by *that*? 'The last ones to see her'. Did you mean 'the last ones to see her *alive*'?"

"I meant what I said. His son was the last person I know of that she talked to. She went with the boy to find his father. That's what I said, and that's what I meant.

"I know you have a job to do. But you think I did something to her. And that is a waste of time."

By that time, my head was spinning. The room I was in looked ancient. And it probably was. The floor was covered in large black and white checkerboard tiles, and when I looked down they seemed to drift apart, draining my life into a deep chasm beneath them.

I needed some caffeine to shake myself from the nightmare I was living.

"*I'll* decide what is and what is not a waste of time," Investigator Pierre barked. "And, yes, we're now *certain* you know what happened to your fiancée. No one, and I mean *no one*, ever saw you or your fiancée at Mass. We know you're lying about that."

I knew that I was a suspect. But to hear those venomous words spewing from the mouth of the man who was appointed to find Jill chewed a monstrous hole through my chest and tore at my heart. I could no longer look into his dark eyes as they pierced my soul.

The lone light above my head and the chipped and dented painted table in front of me I thought were reminiscent of the days of the Bastille. *Could I just be thrown into a French prison and forgotten?*

From that point on I made sure I watched every word I said. And I found it hard even to listen to what he was saying.

"I'm not lying about anything … not now, not ever. Every word I've said has been the truth. I don't give a damn if no one saw me at Mass. Jill and I were there. If you've not been able to find anyone who saw us there, then you're not doing your job! And how about cameras?

"And what I said about her disappearing from Mass—that's true too. You can turn our room upside down, but it's not going to help you find Jill. You are wasting valuable time with this crap."

"Monsieur Martin, I'm the investigator here. And I told you— I'll be the one who decides what is and what is not a waste of time."

"I know that. But you're not going to find the tall man in our closet. And you're not going to find bloody weapons under my bed."

"What do you mean by bloody weapons?"

"I mean, Investigator Pierre, you need to check out surveillance cameras—they must have cameras at Notre Dame. And local hospitals. That's where you should start. If she had an accident or fell and bumped her head, that's where she would be taken. Right?"

"There is nothing to support your story on any video cameras in the area. And we've checked the hospitals. No one by your fiancée's name has been admitted to any of the hospitals in the area."

"Then she was kidnapped …"

"That's Hollywood. That stuff doesn't happen here. Monsieur Martin, you and I both know that you are responsible for your fiancée's disappearance."

I started to interrupt, but the investigator would not allow me to speak.

"Quiet! Let me finish! We've already turned up evidence at your hotel to prove that. All that remains is where and how. The where and how *you* disposed of her body."

He paused for a moment to let his words sink in.

"You could make things easier on yourself if you tell us what happened. Maybe we can lessen the charge. In fact, it would not be out of the question for you to serve your time in the US. And …"

"That's a damn lie. You could not possibly have turned up anything because there is nothing to turn up. I don't know anything about French law, but in the US you'd have to arrest me to keep me, or else let me go. You are inept. You're not doing your job. I wanna get out of here. Now!"

"Well, Monsieur Martin. You're not in New York today. You're in Paris. And we have our own way of doing things. And we can hold you for questioning for as long as we wish."

"You mean there is no such thing as *habeas corpus* in France?"

I did not know what I was talking about. The only thing I knew about *habeas corpus* was what I had seen on TV. I could tell that Investigator Pierre could see through me. It was time for me to shut up before I forced him to apply some obscure French law and have me locked up.

And then it hit me. I do not know where it came from, but for just a moment my mind escaped the confines of Mr. Pierre's interrogation room, and I was transported back to Sugar Island.

It seemed like minutes, but I suspect it was only a few seconds. In that short moment, I could see, taste, and hear the magic of my first date with Jill.

My cousin Janice had set it up. She had met and become best friends with a girl in her creative writing class at Northern Michigan University—that girl was Jill. When my cousin learned that Jill's family had lived on Sugar Island for several generations, she asked her if she knew her cousin Paul.

Janice was stunned to learn that, while Jill had heard of my family name, she had never actually met me. My cousin had grown up in Munising. And even though her family visited mine occasionally during the summers, she never really got to know much about Sugar Island. She assumed that because there were well less than a thousand year-round residents, that we all must know one another.

So my cousin left this message on my voicemail:

"Hey, cousin," she said. "I met this wonderful girl in college. Her name is Jill. She is perfect for you—smart, gorgeous, and, best of all, she lives on Sugar Island. Can you believe that? She's your neighbor, but she says she never met you. Small world! Her last name is Talbot. She's a first-year grad student, so she's a few years younger than you. But she is such a doll. I really want you to meet her.

"So, this is what I've done. She plays the guitar, and she is going to be performing this August, second weekend, at the Sugar Island Music Festival.

"She said that she knows for sure that she will be playing on

Saturday afternoon, the first set after lunch. And that one of the songs is *Sugar Island Girls*.

"I told her that you would wear an NMU cap and be sitting close to the front. It's all outside, so I hope it's not raining.

"After her set she'll come down and meet you. Wish I could be there, but I've got other plans. Don't let me down—Jill's a good friend."

What a day that was. I walked over to take her hand as she was walking off the stage, our eyes met, and I was in love.

"Oh, Monsieur Martin. I see you are a legal expert—"

"No! I'm not. But you are asking me all the wrong questions. You are never going to find Jill like this. I need to get back out there. So, if we're finished, I'd like to go."

"I'll decide when we're done here."

"I'm sure you will. Just arrest me and lock me up. But I'm not talking to you anymore. Not like this."

"Very well, that's exactly what we will do."

"Fine. Do it."

The way he said it convinced me he was bluffing. Had he been sure of himself, he would have immediately led me off and locked me up.

"Please excuse me for a moment, Monsieur Martin. I will confer with my superiors, and we will decide the precise charges. I will be right back. Are you sure you want to go this route?"

"Charge me. Charge me with a crime. And let me call an attorney. Or let me go."

The investigator left me in the room with two other officers. I suspected they were also investigators, but I did not know that for sure. It was obvious that Investigator Pierre had told them not to talk to me, because they had sat there silently the whole time.

Investigator Pierre returned a few minutes later.

"Well, Monsieur Martin," he said. "Good news. My superiors have decided to release you. But do not leave Paris. We are not finished with you."

"I'm not going anywhere without my fiancée. I just wish you would do your job—"

"Be careful, Monsieur Martin, or I might just change my mind," the investigator fired back with a sneer.

I took him at his word and shut up.

"*Au revoir*, Monsieur Martin," he said as we prepared to part. He then extended his hand for me to shake. "Thank you for coming in. I hope my men did not make too big a mess for you."

"No point in making enemies," I reasoned. So I gently squeezed his cold, wet hand. I could not, however, manage a smile.

"Do you need a ride back to your hotel?" he asked.

"No, I'm good." I was not about to give him a chance to change his mind.

"Please help me find my fiancée," I pleaded. "This is unbelievably horrible for me—not to know where she is. If she is okay, or in pain. Or even worse. Please help me."

"Oh, Monsieur Martin. You can rest assured, we *will* find her. Au revoir."

I knew what he was intimating, but I responded pleasantly just the same: "Au revoir."

I was happy to be leaving the building.

Chapter 21

Monday,
12:30 p.m. in Paris

My inclination was to head back to the hotel and come back to the plaza with a bunch of leaflets. I suspected the police had removed all of the original ones. But then I decided against it. The Police Nationale would love to have a simple excuse to lock me up, and disregarding their warning against my placing more notices around Notre Dame would provide them with one. "Even the US Embassy could not get me off on that," I reasoned.

"That's it!" I said loudly enough to be overheard. "I need to go to the US Embassy! Why have I not thought of that before?"

I speed-walked back to the hotel. As I received my key at the desk, I again asked if I had any messages. I was surprised to find that I did—all three of Jill's siblings had called, leaving messages to call them back.

My brother had also called. He said that my doctor had called him. He had apparently been trying to call me, and when he could not reach me, he called my brother. I then recalled that I had left my brother's number with my doctor's office in the event that the office needed to reach me. My brother said he gave the office my email address.

I figured all that could wait. Besides, I did not really want to talk to Jill's family—what could I possibly tell them?

No, the first thing I needed to do was to retrieve our passports from the safe in our room, find the street address for the US Embassy, and then decide if I should walk, take the Metro, or get a taxi.

I momentarily forgot that the Police Nationale had searched my room. While I did notice that some things were not carefully replaced, for the most part, it appeared that they exercised reasonable restraint. It was not as though they "tossed" it, as I had frequently seen done on TV crime shows.

I Googled the embassy's address: 2 Avenue Gabriel, 75008 Paris, France. Entering it on Google Maps, I discovered it was just across the river from Hotel National des Invalides.

"Across from The Invalides," I declared aloud.

I inquired at the front desk as to the preferable means of transportation and was informed that I might use the Metro, or I could take a taxi. I decided this time that I should take a taxi. I felt that taking a bus, or even walking, would give the impression I sensed no urgency. Besides, I needed to conserve my strength.

I checked to be certain both passports were securely tucked into my right pocket, gathered up a handful of posters, and asked the front desk to call for a taxi.

I wrote in large letters across the top of the map I had made, "US Embassy, 2 Avenue Gabriel 75008."

Chapter 22

Monday, 1:55 p.m. in Paris

The memory of the ride to the embassy totally escapes me, but I don't think it took longer than fifteen minutes—fifteen euros (including tip), if measured by cost. My story was regarded like an express ticket. Within a minute of arriving I was ushered into a private office and told to sit down.

"Mr. Martin. My name is Gregory Larson. I've been assigned to help you with your problem."

My first impression of Mr. Larson—thin, tall, fifty-five-ish, divorced, American, with a smell of yesterday's Scotch on his breath. A man who while in college would never have dreamed that an embassy position would someday end up in his obituary.

His desk, cluttered so high that no surface showed through

except on the very edges, told me that he could not possibly name half of the materials placed on it.

Three items, however, had found a substantially flat surface—a shiny silver MacBook Pro, a beige telephone with a twisted cord, and an overloaded ashtray.

He lit up a cigarette without asking if I minded and then entered a few keys on his Mac.

I don't recall much of what immediately followed, only that Mr. Larson requested a great deal of personal information—which I happily provided. And then I recounted the events of the past two days.

I had scribbled the investigator's name down on a used Metro ticket, and I handed it to him.

"He's the investigator handling my case," I said. "I am sure he suspects that I did something to my fiancée. He even ordered that my room be searched."

"And he let you go?"

"Right."

"That means that they didn't find anything incriminating."

"It would be *impossible* to find something incriminating—I've done nothing wrong. Everything I've told them, and you, is the truth. I have nothing to hide."

"I understand. But sometimes when the Police Nationale look hard enough, or want to find evidence badly enough, they turn up something they deem damaging. And that can be enough to detain you indefinitely. It's clear they don't *want* to hold you. That's good."

"The one thing they have against me is my distributing these fliers around Notre Dame. They threatened to arrest me for that."

"Then you should stop. Besides, there are new faces at the cathedral every day. It's not likely that there would be many repeat visitors. But you might want to show the poster to employees—to security in particular."

"I've done that."

"No one remembered her?"

"Right."

"I assume the Police Nationale have a copy of it?"

"Several. But they think I did something to Jill. I don't know how hard they're even looking."

"I'll check with them. But I'm sure they're paying attention to every possible angle. They're very good at their job—especially here in Paris. And especially when there is an American involved."

"Well, they're sure missing something this time."

"I know you are suffering, but I need to ask you a few more questions, including some that might upset you. But we have to know what we're dealing with, especially since this involves the Police Nationale. If they end up with information we don't have, it weakens our ability to help you."

"Ask me anything. I will tell you the truth."

"Very well. Have you or your fiancée ever been arrested, either in France or in the US?"

"Never."

"I'm talking about even a very minor misdemeanor—particularly drugs. Or *anything*, for that matter."

"Never. I've had a couple speeding tickets, but that's it."

"Well, that's certainly unusual. Do you or your fiancée use any nonprescription drugs? Or have you tried to purchase any while in France?"

"We don't use drugs. We've not tried to buy any either."

"Then, when they searched your room, they didn't find any? Is that true? I can't emphasize strongly enough that you level with me. We can't have any surprises down the road."

"Nothing but blood pressure medication, vitamins, Jill probably had some herbal supplements—that's all they could have found."

"Blood pressure medication? Who was that for?"

"I have high blood pressure. My doctor prescribed it."

"That's not a problem. But if you think of anything I should know, something you might have forgotten, just make sure you tell me about it before you leave today.

"Now, I see your passports were stamped Saturday—the day before yesterday, when you entered France. How long are you staying? Do you have your plane ticket to return?"

"We're going home Thursday morning, in less than three days."

I could not help it. Suddenly I was unable to talk or even to think. I just stared unfocused out of the window.

Mr. Larson sat silently for a few moments—he recognized the look.

"I am so sorry, Mr. Martin," he said, handing me a box of tissues. "I can only imagine what you're going through."

I received the tissues from him, thanked him, and eventually set them on the corner of his desk. I wasn't crying.

"I don't know what I'm going to do. I can't leave Paris without her."

"We're going to do everything possible to help you. But I still have some questions I must ask. Are you okay with that?"

"I am. I couldn't sleep last night. And just as I drifted off, the police were at my door. I'm overtired and worried sick. And the Paris police are more interested in blaming me than in finding my fiancée."

"As soon as we finish here, I'll be in contact with them. It's even possible that they've already contacted us. That's doubtful though, because I should have heard if they had. But it is possible.

"Anyway, can we proceed?"

"Sure."

For the next fifteen minutes or so, Mr. Larson continued asking me questions about my relationship with my fiancée—if we had been fighting, if we had a good relationship, if or when we planned to get married. Virtually the same questions the investigator had asked, just in a little less accusatory fashion.

When he was finished, Mr. Larson handed me back our passports.

"I can see that you're very upset. Who wouldn't be? But take these passports and make sure they are secured. If your fiancée has been kidnapped, it will be very difficult to get her out of the country without her passport. Whatever you do, do not surrender either of these passports without first calling me. The number I'm giving you is good twenty-four-seven. If I'm not in the office, I can be tracked down. But just remember, do not surrender them to anyone without first contacting me. Not even to the Police Nationale. I will be in touch as soon as I hear something."

Chapter 23

Monday, 8:00 a.m. on Sugar Island

Jack called his daughter Kate promptly at eight o'clock Monday morning. She, a New York City homicide detective, was not yet in her office, so he left a message.

"Kitty, this is your dad. The sheriff has finally made up his mind to release Reg's body to me. I'm having the funeral home pick him up around ten. As you know, the funeral is scheduled for Wednesday at ten a.m. I am scheduled to arrive in New York at LaGuardia, on Tuesday around seven-fifteen in the evening. If you want to meet me at the airport that would be great. But it would be just as easy for me to take a taxi into the city. I'll be staying at the Midtown Hilton on Sixth Avenue. So maybe we could just meet there around nine-thirty, and we can have a drink. I would like to discuss a few things with you before the funeral. Call me or text me when you get a chance and let me know what you think."

Kate was Jack's only child. Although she was in her thirties, he still considered her his little girl. She was a beautiful young woman by any standards—tall and thin, with the high cheekbones that gave her the appearance of a runway model.

Whenever a friend commented to Jack about his daughter, he was always quick to attribute her beauty to her mother, Jack's deceased wife. In Jack's eyes, however, Kate was more than just his cherished daughter. And it was true. Kate, with her dark eyes and long dark brown hair, bore an amazing resemblance to her mother.

But Kate was more than just a beautiful woman. Kate, with a JD degree from Notre Dame, had worked her way up through the ranks of the New York Homicide Division and was now rumored to be in line for a promotion to lieutenant.

Jack had already told Kate what his schedule was likely to be, but that was before the sheriff had officially informed him that he could have Reg's body.

Jack was confident that if Kate could possibly meet him at the airport, she would do it—especially since it was so late in the evening.

Captain Spencer, Kate's boss, liked her. If he was able to help her, he would. Jack was pretty certain that Kate would at least be able to arrange her schedule so as to join him at the hotel after he'd checked in.

If everything went according to his plan, he would check in, and then they would sit and talk at the Bridges Bar for as long as

Kate wished.

Jack had a number of important matters he needed to discuss with her.

First of all, he wanted to explain to her that it might not be wise for her to attend the funeral. While Reg was Kate's friend too, Jack felt that there were so many negatives attached to his friend's reputation, that Kate as an upwardly mobile New York City homicide detective, might want to reconsider her attendance. For her to be seen associating with the type of characters known to have been a part of Reg's life could tarnish her good standing in the department.

Of course, Jack was fully convinced that she would choose to pay their friend the honor she felt due him, but he felt it only fair to warn her of potential negative repercussions.

Secondly, associates of Allison Fulbright would certainly be there. And Jack knew just how dangerous these people were. They not only posed a risk physically, but they also had the ability to hurt a person politically and socially.

Reg and Kate shared a special bond. Only a year or so had passed since Reg had taken a bullet in a successful effort to free Kate from a group of Eastern European captors. In fact, not only had Reg been instrumental in saving her, but he also had pulled Jack out of the same row house where Kate had been held.

Jack knew that, if given the opportunity, Kate would not be absent from Reg's funeral. Regardless, Jack wanted to warn his daughter.

But there were other things on his mind as well.

Chapter 24

Monday,
3:30 p.m. in Paris

I left the embassy feeling a little better. Even though I did not appreciate some of the questions Mr. Larson asked me, I still believed that he would represent my interests better than I could—and far better than Investigator Pierre and the Police Nationale.

I even felt as though he believed what I told him. I think that was because when I answered one of his questions, he did not fire back with a follow-up question, as the investigator had done.

Of course, it was his job to believe me—or at least to give the appearance of his siding with my cause. But his underlying motivation did not matter to me that much. I was just thankful for his support.

Once outside the embassy gate, I started to walk. I decided to walk all the way back to the hotel. It seemed the appropriate thing to do. First of all, I had no idea how to hail a taxi in Paris. Plus, I thought that the exercise might calm me down and help me to think more clearly. Unfortunately, it took me nearly fifteen minutes before I realized that I was walking west—which was the wrong way.

I abruptly turned and followed the river east until I reached Boulevard Saint-Michel. From there, I knew exactly which side streets to take to get to the hotel. As long as I stayed in sight of the Seine, I was confident that I would not get lost again, no matter my state of mind.

Chapter 25

Monday, 4:57 p.m. in Paris

As I requested my key at the front desk, I again asked for messages. I was surprised that I had one from the investigator. At first I could not discern the caller by looking at it. But the desk clerk read the message to me and explained that it was from the Police Nationale. I then recognized the name of the investigator—known simply to me as Mr. Pierre.

Apparently the US Embassy had contacted him, and he was simply calling me as a courtesy to let me know that.

At least he didn't send officers down here to pick me up this time, I thought. But I was still troubled that he had called. I didn't trust him.

As soon as I walked into the room, a heavy cloud of gloom again confronted me.

I had never before experienced depression. At every other instance in my life, when faced with a seemingly insurmountable problem, I had always been able to turn it into a challenge. That would almost always allow me to wear the problem down to a point of insignificance, or at least diminish its power over me so that time could heal it.

But this time that mode of attack did not even seem available to me.

I knew why I was having difficulty. In times past Jill had always been my anchor. She was the one who would look for the bright side, help develop our plan of action, and then morph into a cheerleader. Her timing was always perfect.

This time I was on my own. And I was finding it impossible to think positive.

"Could it be it?" I asked myself. "*Could* she be dead? Investigator Pierre thinks she is. And even worse than that, *he* thinks I killed her."

While I recognized that this was not a productive approach, sleep deprivation and sheer panic pushed me into that corner.

I had heard that in the case of missing persons you have forty-eight hours to work with. If a person does not turn up during that time, the outcome would almost always be bad.

I started counting on my fingers—one full day, plus four hours. Jill had now been missing twenty-eight hours. And compounding the problem, I did not believe the Police Nationale was giving her situation its best effort.

After I had secured the passports in the safe, I turned to my emails—I had new messages from all three of Jill's siblings as well as from others.

As always, her sisters had to come first.

I opened my MacBook and logged onto the Internet. It made the most sense to communicate with them using email. Again I sent the same message to her family members.

"Had a long interview with the Police Nationale this morning. Can't say it went well but was hopefully beneficial to them. I then went to the US Embassy. They were very nice and promised to do what they could. The representative I met with, Mr. Gregory Larson, said he would contact the Police Nationale and work with their investigation."

I knew I needed to radiate an air of confidence, even though I was far from feeling it.

"Mr. Larson gave me a lot of good advice. One of the things he said was that the Police Nationale was a highly professional organization and that their investigators would not rest until they got to the bottom of your sister's disappearance.

"I have not slept well, so I am going to try to get a little rest before I continue. About the only things I can do are to keep after the investigator and continue talking to workers at Notre Dame. I will email you again as soon as I hear anything. Love—Paul."

This was not the time for long emails. I had nothing good to report, and they could easily see that.

I then remembered that Jenny had included in her earlier message that there was an emergency email that I needed to read. Scrolling through my messages, I found it. It was from my doctor's email address.

What could that be? I wondered.

Just before we left for Paris I had visited his office on Jill's insistence to have the doctor check out what I thought was a harmless mole. He seemed to agree with me that it appeared benign but said he would feel better if he sent it over to the lab to be sure.

I counted back six hours and determined that his office would not yet be open. So I emailed him: "We are in Paris, and phones are not readily available to me. I'm thinking that the results must be in from the biopsy, so if you could please email them to me, that would be nice. I know that is not protocol, but it would work best for me under these circumstances."

That left the call to the investigator. "I do not want to call that man," I muttered.

We did not like each other, or at least I didn't like him. I wanted to get some sleep, and if I talked to him right now, sleep in the near future could be very elusive.

"I wonder if his email address is on his card?" I said aloud.

It was. And I did:

"Dear Investigator Tiffeneau— I met with the US Embassy this afternoon. The man I talked to, a Mr. Gregory Larson, offered his assistance to your office. He said you should feel free to call him if you wish. With regard to your request for me to call you, I do not have a cell phone. Jill and I were both using hers. If you could possibly email me what you need, I would be happy to respond. Or if you want me to come down to your office again, I would also be happy to do that. Do you have anything new?"

After I hit the "Send" button, I got to thinking, *What if he has some news about Jill ... I'm going to have to call him.*

I immediately rang the front desk and asked them to put a call through to Mr. Pierre. But just as they were about to dial his number, an email came in from him.

"Hold on," I said. "Cancel that call. I just got an email from the investigator."

I clicked on the email.

"Nothing yet. I did hear from Mr. Larson at the US Embassy. He offered his help. I just wanted to let you know that."

Chapter 26

Monday, 6:02 p.m. in Paris

Milk, with peanut butter on bread—that should help me sleep tonight. While we did not have a refrigerator in the room, it was late summer. So we bought a box of processed milk and kept it cool on the ledge outside the front window. I poured a glass, laid out three small slices of bread on a paper towel, and judiciously spread on them the creamy Jif I had brought to Paris in my check-in luggage. I ate them slowly.

Jill had left her iPad charging, so I found her "white noise" application, turned it on, and cranked the volume all the way up. It masked virtually all the street racket.

Thankfully, the room had very thick drapery, as well as sheers. When I closed them, it blocked out all light.

I was beginning to feel a little like Al Pacino in *Insomnia.*

I checked the phone one last time to be sure I had not missed any messages from the front desk.

The milk and carbs performed as expected. It seemed like only minutes had passed, but I knew I had slept. It was almost as though someone had hit me on the head and knocked me out.

Chapter 27

Tuesday, 1:33 a.m. in Paris

It was almost two in the morning when I awoke. I had slept a little less than eight straight hours.

The first thing I did after turning on a light was to turn off the white noise. I then checked emails. All the siblings had sent messages again. So I responded to each of them in order. Even though I had not heard from the police or the embassy, I felt it was imperative to communicate something: "I have no news. I did get some sleep, thank God. It is now two in the morning here. Not much I can do right now. I will be in touch later today and right away if I learn anything."

I called down and checked for telephone messages. My call startled the desk clerk—I think he'd been sleeping. He checked and found none. Hopefully, he hadn't been sleeping *all* night.

Just before I logged off, I spotted a message from my doctor. I had not been expecting an email from him, and so I almost overlooked it.

"Hello, Paul. This is Dr. Rogers. I never like to email test results, but the current situation dictates that I must inform you regarding the results of your biopsy as soon as possible. The tests indicate that the tumor I removed just before your trip was malignant. Given the fact that over the past two years I have removed two previous malignant tumors from different parts of your body, I would like you to come in when you get back so we can check to see if we're missing anything. There is every reason to think that I got all of it, and given the fact that it was relatively thin (at worst stage IIA), there is no reason to think that it metastasized. As soon as you get back, give my office a call and we will set up a visit. Enjoy the rest of your vacation, and we will deal with it when you get back."

I knew what that meant. Nine years ago my mother had fielded a similar call from my younger brother's doctor: melanoma, stage II. One year later we had his funeral.

I will admit that somewhere, tugging on my brain, I had suspected I would develop skin cancer, just as my brother had suffered. Not only was it part of my family history, but we'd both spent a lot of time in the sun when we were children.

I sat back in my chair and closed my eyes. "How ironic is this?" I muttered. I had already considered this to be a bit of a "bucket list" trip, but for a different reason—an impending major operation on my heart. Jill and I had wanted to spend some pleasant time in Paris before I had the surgery to repair it.

The procedure I needed was a complicated one. Even though

there was typically a high level of success resulting from the operation, it required stopping my heart for a lengthy period of time, mechanically pumping blood to my brain and to the rest of my body, and then replacing the aortic valve, the ascending aorta, the arch, and the descending aorta. My choice of words might not be scientific, but they accurately convey the notion just the same.

Too many things could go wrong, I thought.

What if the new vessel leading to my brain constricted the blood flow? I would lose my mental edge.

Adding to my concern was the fact that my nephew had undergone a similar operation, and as a result he'd lost a noticeable degree of his mental capabilities.

I did not know what to expect. In fact, I questioned whether or not I wanted to get married at all, given the negative possibilities associated with this type of procedure.

So, we decided to get this trip to Paris in while I was still physically strong and able to think straight. When we returned we would make our plans for the future.

Of course, the doctors warned against the trip.

The heart surgeon was outspokenly opposed: "You have two months at the most before that aneurysm starts to leak or totally gives out," he said. "And when it happens, the only way you survive is if it gives out in an emergency room. I'd give you two weeks to two months, if that."

"Well," I chuckled as I sat alone in my room. "At least now I won't have to go under the knife to fix my heart."

For some strange reason I felt a sense of relief—perhaps of the comic variety.

"How weird is that?" I said smiling. "Apparently I have been dreading the surgery more than I feared death."

In fact, that's exactly how my attorney viewed it. While help-ing me do all the things a person in my condition has to do to prepare for all contingencies, such as setting up a trust and writing a will, he blurted out, "Paul, you're just too busy to die."

"I need a cup of coffee," I quipped to myself.

Here I was in Paris, in the middle of the night. I did not like it. Maybe that's why I started talking to myself. Maybe that's what I had been doing all along—talking to myself. Perhaps I just liked hearing myself talk.

Even before Jill disappeared, when we would be alone in the evening, I would just keep talking. Jill would always respond, and we would converse, but perhaps I just liked hearing myself talk. That's a real possibility because right now she wasn't here, and I still couldn't quit talking.

We had brought a French press to Paris, and a one-pound bag of Starbucks ground dark espresso. My intention was to boil water every morning and French press a batch of breakfast coffee. We would each have a cup, and I would then put the rest in a small stainless steel thermos.

Why should today be different?

Nothing had really changed from the day before. Jill was still missing, and I still had to look for her. That's all that mattered. While the email from my doctor provided information regarding my physical condition that I had lacked the day before, the truth is that only my knowledge of it had changed. I was no worse off that day than I had been before. Besides, I had already suspected I had cancer.

So, I reasoned, *I made it through yesterday okay. I can make it through today as well.*

I folded a sheet of clean paper in half, found a pen, and sat down with a cup of fresh brew. That's just how Jill and I started every day—with a cup of coffee and an analog itinerary.

Chapter 28

Tuesday, 1:38 a.m. in Paris

We were scheduled to catch our plane at twelve-fifteen p.m. on Thursday—in roughly fifty-seven and a half hours. I drew a horizontal line through the middle of the sheet, put *Today* on the top, and then underlined it.

Just below the horizontal line I wrote *Tomorrow* and underlined it as well. I flipped the paper over and wrote *Thursday* on the top of the other side. Under *Today*, I wrote, *Confirm Shuttle with*

Front Desk.

When we first checked in we talked to the front desk about arranging for a taxi to get us back to the airport on Thursday. At that time, Claire suggested the shuttle because it would cost less. Both Jill and I thought it sounded like the right thing to do, but I was not sure we had formally requested the service.

They liked to have a three-day reservation. So, if our request had not actually been finalized earlier, it could present a problem. I needed to confirm.

Next, I wrote *Call Police.*

By creating a list like this, it made performing the tasks much easier. I thought of them as commands—orders handed down by an unnamed higher power.

I dropped down the page and wrote *Call Police* under the tasks for tomorrow as well. And under that heading for both days, I wrote *Call Embassy.*

I thought for a moment and then wrote *Print Fliers* and *Visit Notre Dame*, again for both days.

There was very little I could do on my own to find Jill, except for performing those tasks daily.

There, I thought. *I've got the mandatories out of the way. Now I can concentrate on the electives.*

I sipped my coffee. And then, leaving as much white space as possible, I wrote at the very bottom of the page, under the *Tomorrow* heading, *Pack up.*

That would be very difficult to do—especially packing Jill's belongings. I had never packed for her, but I would need to this time.

After thinking silently for a few moments, I wrote at the bottom of my *Today* list, *Love Lock.* Some time, before I went to bed on this day, I would take a walk down to the Love Lock Bridge.

Actually, there are two Love Lock bridges in Paris. The first one is a pedestrian bridge across the Seine. The bridge connects the Institut de France, on the south side of the Seine, to the Louvre on the north. Its real name is Pont des Arts. The bridge has been featured in numerous cinematic productions such as *Amelie* and *Le Pont des Arts*. It was unofficially renamed Love Lock by romantic couples who attached padlocks to it, symbolizing their undying love. After securing the lock, the lovers would kiss and then toss the keys to the lock in the Seine.

Jill discovered the bridge's tradition on a television travel program, and we thought that it would be awesome to attach our own lock.

While there were street vendors selling touristy locks at the bridge, we felt that we needed a more proper lock. So, before we left on the trip, we found the *perfect* solid brass padlock at Lock City Home Center in Sault Ste. Marie and had it engraved: "Paul and Jill—forever lovers."

So, on Saturday, our first day in Paris on this trip, Jill and I prepared to do the deed. On the way into the city from the airport, we told our English-speaking taxi driver about our plans to affix our lock on the Love Lock Bridge. He told us that there recently had been a problem with the city regarding the original Love Lock Bridge, the Pont des Arts. Members of the Paris government had threatened to have the locks removed.

Possibly because of that controversy, or more likely due to overfilling, there became a second Love Lock bridge—this was the Pont de l'Archeveche Bridge, located across the Seine, directly behind Notre Dame. Every available inch of this new Love Lock

Bridge had now also been covered with padlocks—many thousands of them. Some lovers had even begun attaching their locks to the locks of others, due to lack of space.

We chose this bridge over Pont des Arts largely because it was located close to our hotel.

We were staying in the Latin Quarter, which made the location of the Pont de l'Archeveche perfect for us.

We had arrived at our hotel around eight a.m. Saturday. By eleven a.m. we were on our way to the bridge.

The lock I had purchased was perfect. Even though there was little room left on the bridge to attach it, we were able to slide its exceptionally long shackle through a hole and then draw it back and click it closed.

We made sure before latching it that it would settle in right side up—so the inscription could easily be read.

Once it was securely locked, we kissed, and together we dropped the keys into the Seine. I'm sure it's against the law to throw anything into the river, but nearly ten thousand other couples had done the same thing, and I hadn't heard about any of those other lovers being arrested.

Jill took pictures of the lock and emailed them to our friends and relatives. We joked about it being almost like a destination wedding—just much cheaper.

I then calculated and logged its distance from the nearest light post, so we could find it on future visits.

We then walked down the Seine to the Petit Point Bridge. It was cold—barely above freezing. None of the bookstalls (*les bouquinistes*) were yet open.

The stalls have been a permanent fixture along the river for centuries. Every afternoon merchants begin unlocking the steel-hinged lids that covered their stalls, exposing bins of books and magazines, many dating from the nineteenth century. During the warmer months, every stall is opened. But in weather like this, fewer than half of the merchants bothered, and those that did maintain an abbreviated schedule.

We talked about returning later that day but decided it would be best to retire to our hotel and get some sleep. It might have been noon on the clock, but our bodies knew it was really only six a.m.

Perhaps it would be warmer tomorrow, we hoped.

As I sat there writing my list for the day, I realized I was smiling. Reminiscing about the quest of securing our lock on the bridge, all the associated significance induced a tear-fighting smile.

Tonight, I thought, *after it gets dark, I will go down and find the lock one more time.*

By the time Jill went missing, she and I had already stopped twice to verify that our lock was still there and that we could readily find it. We had talked about repeating our Love Lock visits every year until we ran out of money.

I sat on the corner of my bed, numbly staring into space.

What else could I possibly put on my list? I wondered. And then I wrote *Do Emails* for both days.

I then skipped to the bottom of the *Tomorrow* list and wrote *Love Lock* on it as well.

"Why not?" I asked aloud.

Once I had written that, my future was set. Now all I would have to do was complete my appointed tasks and then cross them off. That was, after all, why we made these evolving lists in the first place—for the satisfaction of crossing off entries after completion.

These lists ensured a regret-free life.

I brushed my teeth and went down to the main desk.

"Yes," the desk clerk said, "we have you on the list for a shuttle at eight a.m. on Thursday."

Chapter 29

Tuesday,
2:52 a.m. in Paris

I returned to the room and drew a line through "Shuttle."
Next on my schedule was calling the police. As before, I did not want to talk to the investigator. And I certainly did not want to go down there again. So I simply emailed him. "Just checking in to see how your investigation was going. Please call my hotel with anything or if you need me to do something."

I then crossed off "Call Police."

My next task was to call the embassy. That I didn't mind. I had the front desk dial the number. I gave them my name and asked for Gregory Larson.

Because it was so early, I expected his voicemail. I was shocked when he answered. Apparently he had requested his office to forward any calls from me through to his cell phone.

"Mr. Martin," he said. "This is Gregory Larson. Thank you for calling. I wanted you to know that I have been in contact with the investigator in charge of your case, Pierre Tiffeneau, and he assured me it had his full attention."

"He did let me know you had called him."

"That's good. It's important that you maintain a line of communication with him. Now, as it turns out, I actually know this investigator personally. I think he is the principal English-speaking liaison in the investigative department. So, when the Police Nationale has occasion to work with an American, most often he is the investigator involved.

"I have found him to be very professional, and fair. We have had a good working relationship. I do not get the impression at all that he suspects only you. He expressed great concern that your fiancée is missing in Paris. He is very troubled about that. But he is probably the best person in Paris to have working on the case."

"That's good to hear because I certainly did not get that impression."

"He's a cop. It's his job to be tough—perhaps even to instill a bit of fear. But he's a good cop. I will be calling him later today. We've got to get something resolved because you're planning to go back to the US on Thursday. Isn't that right?"

"Our ticket is for Thursday at twelve-fifteen p.m."

"What are your contingency plans? If we've not found your fiancée."

"I have none."

"That's only two days away. I think you should talk to your hotel and make arrangements to stay beyond that date if you have to. I don't think you should try to leave the country with this pending."

I can't remember anything else that was said, except for the perfunctory "thank you and goodbye."

The prospect of prolonging my stay had never crossed my mind.

Nevertheless, after I printed up a dozen fliers with Jill's picture and info, I crossed off *Call Embassy* and *Print Fliers,* and I went down to talk to the desk clerk.

"I just talked to my embassy," I said to the clerk. "The embassy suggested that I should talk to you about possibly staying another week. Would that be a problem?"

Everyone who worked at the hotel was aware of my plight. He assured me that the hotel would work with me in every way possible. Besides, it was the off-season, and they had rooms available. They said I might have to switch to a different room, but they could work something out for me if it turned out that I would have to extend my stay.

That was a relief. I could now drop the subject and focus on talking to Notre Dame employees.

Today:
Schedule Shuttle
Call Police
Call Embassy
Distribute Fliers at Notre Dame
Love Lock
Do Emails

Tomorrow:

Call Police

Call Embassy

Distribute Fliers at Notre Dame

Do Emails

Love Lock

Pack up

Thursday: Head back home

Chapter 30

Tuesday, 10:00 a.m. in Paris

I was surprised when Notre Dame security immediately ushered me into their administrator's office. There I met Archard Durand—the head of security.

He was a tall, very thin man—probably fifty years of age. He wore an expensive navy blue pinstripe, with a stiffly starched white shirt, dark blue tie, and black well-polished shoes.

He stood to shake my hand as I was presented to him. It was a firm, warm handshake, which, with a sincere smile, immediately put me at ease.

I was surprised by his subdued manner. After my experience with Investigator Pierre, I was expecting the worst. Instead, Monsieur Durand struck me more like a French version of David Niven. His neatly groomed black hair showed a little gray on his temples. But I think it was his reserved version of a Dali mustache that best defined his appearance.

If I were to guess, I would say that in his youth he had either attended seminary or at least contemplated it. His eyes showed warmth, and his actions suggested he was a man of compassion.

After greeting me, he immediately prepared coffee in his French press. He didn't ask me if I cared for a cup. He poured it, and then, using both hands, he presented it to me in a ceramic mug that bore the insignia "ND."

"Monsieur Martin," he said. "I would like to make you a gift of this mug, if you would like to have it."

His English was excellent. He explained to me that a member of the Police Nationale (probably my investigator, I reasoned) had already met with him and presented him with several black and white copies of the color flier. That was encouraging, except for the fact that the Police Nationale had blacked out my hotel's phone number and replaced it with theirs.

I wrote the hotel's phone number beside that of the Police Nationale.

When he saw the much clearer image of Jill, he asked for some of the fliers I had made, and he immediately tacked one to his corkboard.

I sensed that he was trying to placate me. But that was okay. At least he didn't toss me out. And I am a firm believer in the concept that the squeaky wheel gets the grease. At least he made me think I was making an impact.

He did request that I not distribute any more of them in the cathedral. I agreed not to, even though I had every intention of coming back with more on Wednesday. After all, Notre Dame was on my list for Wednesday as well.

His words effectively put an end to my efforts at the cathedral for this day. For, were I to stay and hand out fliers at Notre Dame, I would be violating my word not to do so.

I thanked him and made sure he had the hotel phone number. Of course, it was already printed on the fliers I had given him.

I followed him closely as he walked me out of the main office complex. In spite of his kind words and sincere concern, my heart was deeply saddened.

When we reached the huge outside door, he held it open for me and again offered me his hand to shake.

"Monsieur Martin," he said. "It was a pleasure to meet you. I am just sorry that it had to be under such unpleasant circumstances."

He then paused for a moment but did not release my hand. "Do you know the history of this wonderful cathedral? Did you know that through the centuries many peoples sought to plunder its treasures and to bring about its destruction?

"Yet, in the end it came through stronger than ever. I wish that for you—that you and your fiancée will emerge after this awful event, stronger than ever. And that you will enjoy a long life with this wonderful woman whom you love."

I smiled back, even though I was fighting off tears, and thanked him. I thoroughly believed that if he heard anything at all, Monsieur Durand would promptly follow up on it.

However, his call would be to the Police Nationale, not to me. I was not pleased about that because I had no doubts about how Investigator Pierre felt about me.

Chapter 31

Tuesday, 11:00 a.m. in Paris

I did feel a little better knowing that he at least was cognizant of the matter.

It was much too early to go back to the hotel, so I turned east out of the cathedral and took a walk on the north side of the Seine, over to the Love Lock Bridge.

I found our landmark light pole and paced off twelve feet toward the center of the bridge. And there it was: "Paul and Jill—forever lovers." I knelt down and touched it.

"Excuse me, sir," a young man said. "Do you speak English?"

"Yes."

"Would you take a picture of my girlfriend and me?" he said, reaching forward to hand his camera to me.

"Sure, where would you like to stand?"

He searched around until he found their lock and said, "Right here. Could you stand so you can get Notre Dame in the background?"

"Sure."

I pointed the camera and shot.

"Here, check it out. Be sure it's good."

He looked at the image and replied, "It's great. Thank you so much."

I smiled and said, "It was a pleasure."

Looking around, I realized that there were half a dozen couples waiting for someone to take their pictures. While I was happy to add my blessing to their commitment, I was so near desperation that all I wanted to do right then was to take a Forrest Gump type walk. And so I did.

I exited the bridge on the south end and proceeded down the river until I reached the Musée d'Orsay. I leaned back on the river wall and admired the architecture. The walk covered only a mile or so, but it was enough to clear my head a bit.

I decided to head back to the hotel, check for messages, and reorganize.

Chapter 32

Tuesday, 7:45 a.m. on Sugar Island

Y es, it is. And good morning to you."

"I am sorry to call this early, but the caller says it's an emergency."

"That's fine. I was awake and having a cup of coffee," Jack said. "Go ahead and put him through."

"*Her*, Jack. The caller is a female. And thanks, I'll put her through."

"Good morning, Mr. Handler. This is Lesley Wallace. I'm a neighbor here on the island."

"Of course, Mrs. Wallace. And you were Red's favorite teacher. He raved about you all last year. Everything's okay with Red's school? Red is looking forward to the new school year."

"Everything is fine with school. This is purely a personal matter. You can just tell me whether or not you think you can help me or even advise me. I would appreciate anything you can do, and if you don't have anything to say, I'll even understand that. My husband says that I'm making a mountain out of a molehill anyway. I really don't know. But I've heard so much about you. I would at least like you to tell me what I should do—if anything."

"I'll do what I can. What's the problem? And please call me Jack."

"Then you have to call me Lesley."

Lesley, besides being one of Red's favorite schoolteachers, had become well known in the Upper Peninsula as a writer of poetry. During the summers, she was in demand as a reader at libraries and writers groups. Several of her poems had been set to music, and some had been recorded by popular artists.

"That works, Lesley. Now tell me a little bit about your dilemma."

"My sister Jill and her fiancé are in Paris. And when she travels we always exchange emails, every day.

"We just received a very disturbing email from Paul, Jill's boyfriend, and apparently Jill went missing on Sunday."

"In *Paris*? Do you know where she was staying, or where she was when she went missing?"

"According to Paul, Jill disappeared from Notre Dame, during a Mass."

"And she's been missing since Sunday?" Jack said. "That's over two full days. And no one's heard *anything*?"

"No. Nothing at all. And my sister always does a good job at staying in touch. Since our mom died we sisters have grown closer. Or maybe we just lean on each other more. She does travel a lot, but she always calls or emails me. I mean, this time, not even her fiancé knows where she is. We've been emailing back and forth about it with Paul."

Jack thought for a moment and then asked, "How do they get along? Your sister and her fiancé? Have they ever split up? Do they seem to have a lot of fights? It's important that you don't hold anything back. I need to know the whole truth, even if it's a little embarrassing. When this all blows over, we'll both forget that you ever told me these things. But right now I need to know as much as you do."

"They don't fight any more than anyone else—I'd say they get along *very* well. But back to something you just said—you talked about it blowing over. Do you think it *will* blow over?"

"These things usually sort themselves out. Eventually."

"That's what my husband says. Then you would agree with him?"

"I'm not suggesting that. To me, this sounds very suspicious. We should continue to hope for the best. And even *expect* the best. But we must also consider the fact that your sister is in a foreign country. And because of that alone she is at a substantial disadvantage."

"Are you saying that you will help me?"

"I'll poke around a little and see what I can come up with. Why don't you give me your other sister's name and her phone number. When we hang up you should call her so she is expecting my call.

Is she likely to be home right now?"

"I'm not sure about that—she was an hour ago. I'll give you her cell and her office number—one of them should work. When will you call me back, to let me know what you find?"

Lesley gave Jack her cell phone number as well as two numbers for Jenny.

Jack asked her for email addresses as well as phone numbers, just in case he would not be able to reach them on the phone, and he informed her that he would communicate primarily through emails. If, however, he had specific news or needed additional information, then he would call.

Chapter 33

Tuesday, 7:50 a.m. on Sugar Island

The first thing Jack did was to call Jenny Talbot, Jill's younger sister. She was home.

"Hello. This is Jack Handler. I'm a friend of Lesley Wallace. She asked me to give you a call and let you know I would be trying to get hold of your sister Jill. I believe that she and her fiancé are vacationing in Paris right now. And that she, your sister Jill, has gone missing. Is that about right?"

"Hello, Mr. Handler. Lesley just called. She told me you lived here on Sugar Island as well. Funny how it's such a small place, yet there are so many people who live here, or *have* lived here. Lesley told me you'd be giving me a call. Thank you so much for helping us."

"It is your sister that you can't reach?" Jack asked. "Is that right?"

"That's right, but we really can't reach Paul either—at least not by phone. They had one cell phone, and it's gone. We've been emailing Paul. And we have the phone number at the hotel. But we've not been able to talk to him. We have communicated using email. We think that maybe he doesn't understand how to make an international call. He's been faithful with the emails, however."

"Could you fill me in on what's going on, as best you can?"

"Paul writes that he and my sister were at Notre Dame for Mass. Apparently Jill got up to help a lost boy find his father. And that's the last Paul saw her.

"He's got the police involved, *and* the US Embassy. But so far nothing's come of it."

Jenny then broke down and began to cry. She was the youngest of the siblings. And while the girls were all very close, she and Jill were especially so, with Jill doing her best to fill the void left when their mother had passed away.

"Paul loves my sister so much. And he has a serious heart condition. I don't know how well he could be handling this. Please. Please, Mr. Handler. *Please* try to help us."

"What do you mean by that—a heart condition? How old is he?"

"He's thirty, I think. Not very old for that sort of thing. I think it's hereditary. His father passed away when he was quite young—from heart disease. None of us are really sure as to the exact nature of it—he doesn't talk about it. Jill just said that the doctors told them that Paul really needed to have an operation to fix it. But he and Jill wanted to take this trip first."

Jack also wanted to ask Jenny if the couple fought much. But he thought better of it, given the obvious fragile state of her emotions right then. For now he had to assume that a young woman was missing and that her fiancé was doing his best to find her.

Nevertheless, nagging on his mind was the fact that in most instances such as this, it is the lover or the husband who is directly responsible for a woman's disappearance. And, fair or unfair, Jack knew that just like in any big city, the Paris police were going to make that same assumption.

They're not going to expend much energy looking for this woman for at least a few days, he concluded. *And then, when they do get serious, they're going to focus on the fiancé. I do not envy this Paul guy one bit—especially given the language barrier.*

Jack then assured Jenny that he would do his best to get the matter resolved—but it was going to be very difficult to make progress from this side of the Atlantic.

It was at this point that Jack first began to consider the possibility that he might need to go to Paris to properly resolve this matter.

He read the email address he had for Paul to confirm that it was correct, and then again tried to reassure the sister. "Jenny, I will see what I can come up with. I will touch base with you soon, whether or not I make progress. Please let me know *immediately* if you learn anything. I can't stress enough that if you hear anything, and I do mean *anything*, that you let me know as soon as possible. Even if it doesn't seem important to you."

As soon as he disconnected the call, he sent an email to Paul, basically reiterating the conversation he had just had with Jenny, asking Paul to give him a call as soon as possible to discuss the status of his fiancée.

Chapter 34

Tuesday, 8:06 a.m. on Sugar Island

Jack was very concerned about the disappearance of the Sugar Island girl in Paris. Had it not been imperative that he be present at his friend's funeral, Jack would happily have made reservations on the first flight available to CDG International Airport. Even though Jack had attempted to mitigate the severity of the situation for the benefit of the family, he knew that this young neighbor was in serious trouble.

Seldom did Jack seek favors from his daughter. But this was going to be the exception. And so much for his seeking to convince Kate that she ought to pass on Reg's funeral. Now, Jack needed Kate's help, and he needed her to meet him at the funeral.

Jack had made reservations on US Airways flight 1775 departing from LaGuardia on Wednesday at 3:35 p.m. and arriving in

Paris on Thursday at 7:55 a.m.

Because the funeral was scheduled for ten a.m., he knew that it would make for a very tight schedule. So he was planning to have Kate drive him directly from Calvary Cemetery to LaGuardia. He could see no other alternative.

He would check out of the Hilton before the funeral and remain at the funeral only until Reg was buried. He would take a moment to console Pam, Reg's widow, and then he would bolt.

He would have asked Roger Minsk, his friend in the Secret Service, to drive him to the airport, but Roger had earlier informed him that Allison had requested to meet with him immediately after the funeral.

So, Kate became Jack's logical choice.

He knew that if anyone could get him to LaGuardia in time to catch the plane, she could use her siren and lights to do it.

Jack would have her swing into the cemetery and pick him up, and then right back out again. Traffic on a Wednesday at noon should not be a problem. And if she used her lights and siren, they should be able to make it by twelve-thirty—or at least before one.

That should work.

All he had to do would be to convince Kate that she needed to do this favor for him.

As soon as he had finished his message to Kate, Jack called the local funeral home to inform them that they could pick up Reg's body from the morgue any time after ten and prepare it for transport to New York on Tuesday afternoon.

And just as he had finished giving them instructions, his cell phone vibrated—it was Kate.

Given a choice between texting and straight conversation, Jack would always choose conversation and voice messages over texting.

Even when Kate would text him, Jack would call her back rather than reply via a return text.

Kate once teased him about his texting skills. "How will you ever learn how to text and drive if you can't key your phone without looking?" she asked him.

"I can't even talk on my phone and drive, much less text and drive," he replied.

While Jack was getting more proficient at texting, it was only out of necessity. Red, his nephew, who was physically unable to speak due to an earlier injury to his voice box, was forcing Jack to learn how to text. Still, even though he was *technically* texting, what he was doing could be called that only because he was using the texting function, the language he used was largely one of his own invention. Kate teased him about that as well.

"Dad," she said. "I got your message. You'd like me to meet you at the airport Tuesday evening? Or should I go directly to the hotel and catch you there?"

"Whichever works best for you," he replied. "Might actually be best if you went directly to the hotel, because traffic will still be a bear at that time."

"That's what I was thinking. What time do you expect to get to the hotel?"

"Traffic won't be so bad coming into the city at that time, so I'd guess I'll get there sometime around nine."

"I'll just hang out at the precinct for a while, catch up on my paperwork, and then plan on getting to the hotel about nine. I'll take a taxi. Shall I meet you in the bar after you check in?"

"That sounds good."

"And about the funeral," Kate said. "I take it you don't want me to go to it. Rather you'd like me to pick you up there after the funeral and drive you to the airport?"

"Exactly. I'll ride there with Roger. And if you get there at noon, we can make it to LaGuardia in time for my flight."

"That's the part that puzzles me," Kate said. "What's that all about?"

"One of our neighbors on Sugar Island has gone missing in Paris," he explained. "Her sister, who also lives on the island, asked me if I could help locate her. Actually, the sister is one of Red's teachers—his favorite teacher, in fact."

"Missing in Paris?" Kate repeated.

"Long story," Jack said. "Could be … hell, probably will be … that she will most likely turn up safe and sound, somewhere in Paris, and I can cancel the trip. But, as it stands right now, it's still on for Wednesday afternoon."

"Not if you forget your passport," Kate teased him.

"I've already packed it," Jack replied. "Maybe you should take a few days off and go with me."

"Can't. I have to be in court for a prelim on one of my collars. It's one of those cases that ought to plead out, but it doesn't look like it will. The fellow's attorney wants the trial experience, I think. He doesn't have a case. He's treating it like a traffic citation, like he thinks I might not show up or something. I think it's his first big case."

"Can't the prosecutor make him an offer he can't refuse? If you asked him nice?"

"Already have, and he turned it down. It seems as though he

wants to drag it out and hope for a miracle."

"What's it about? Who's the attorney?" Jack asked.

"The firm is based out of your old hometown—Chicago."

"Really?" Jack queried. "What's the firm?"

"Smith, Smith, and Rolly. Ever heard of it?"

"Hell yes!" Jack said. "That's the most prestigious law firm in Chicago. You've heard the term 'white-shoe law firm?' Well, Smith, Smith, and Rolly fits that bill better than any other law firm in the Midwest. Who exactly *is* this defendant?"

"His name is Randall Croft—Randall James Croft. Ever heard of him?"

"I'm aware of his reputation," Jack said. "What's the nature of his alleged crime?"

"You know," Kate said, "now that you suggest that he's being represented by a big firm, it makes me wonder. This guy was arrested along with his two daughters. But for some reason, the daughters are being tried separately. And it involves the same crime."

"Describe the daughters," Jack said. "Do you know what they look like?"

"Yeah. I haven't seen them, but they're supposed to be quite beautiful."

"Shit," Jack said. "Who did they supposedly kill?"

"It was a simple robbery, apparently. The girls lured the victim into a hotel room, and the father came in and killed him."

"*Simple* robbery?" Jack questioned. "You think it was a simple robbery?"

"I do, and I think you might have heard of him—the VIC. He used to work in the Fulbright White House. His last name was

Williams, but he was known by insiders simply as Steve. He was one of those guys known almost exclusively by first name only. Like Elvis. He served President Fulbright as an advisor. I think his area of expertise was in promotion. He was reputedly a genius when it came to handling the press."

Of course, Jack knew exactly about whom she was talking—Steve, Allison's friend. Jack also knew him by his first name only. He was one of the six original co-conspirators in Allison's failed assassination plot. Now that Steve was dead it meant that the only surviving members of the conspiracy were Allison and Jack, a position Jack rightly concluded was not enviable for either one of them.

Jack was familiar with the handiwork of the Croft family—a father and his three children, two daughters and a son. He was certain that it was this group that Allison had sent to Sugar Island earlier to kill the two lawyers Pam Black had dispatched to see Jack. The purpose of that visit was to enlist Jack's help in blocking Allison's attempt to have Reg's body exhumed.

The Croft family had managed to murder the two lawyers in broad daylight on the Sugar Island Ferry. And no one saw them do it.

Jack knew they were very talented at what they did. And he knew that Kate's life was in danger as this murder case made its way through the New York court system.

Jack could not explain to Kate under what circumstances he knew this Steve without giving away information that could be very dangerous to them both.

"How is it you have to testify against him?" Jack asked.

"I'm the one who tracked him down," she replied. "I was with my officers when we made the arrest at Kennedy. He was headed to Florida—Ft. Lauderdale."

"And the daughters, were they with him?"

"No," Kate said. "They were arrested in Newark getting on a plane, also headed to Ft. Lauderdale, same as their father."

"And they're being tried separately?"

"Right, but not for murder, at least not yet," Kate said. "We notified New Jersey. I just had a hunch. And the Newark PD, with the help of the Feds, arrested them getting on a plane. But, New Jersey didn't want to release them to us because they thought our case might fall apart, so they are holding them on some older charges. Apparently the two girls had failed to appear after they had been subpoenaed. It was like a four-year-old case, and they were only witnesses. But New Jersey liked their chances of getting a conviction a little better than they liked our case."

"I think New Jersey might have known something about this Croft guy," Jack said. "He has a reputation for being very difficult to convict of anything. If you run his NCIC I'll bet you'll come up with a long list of arrests but few convictions, if any."

"Exactly," Kate said. "Then you *do* know him?"

"I know *about* him," Jack said. "He is a very high-priced mechanic—he's a gun for hire. And he only works for elite clients. People who are well connected, and *very* well financed. Kitty, if there is any way you can separate yourself from this case, you should do it. This Croft guy, and the people he works for—they are very dangerous. There's a good reason, a very good reason, that he has never been convicted of anything. I strongly advise you to seek to distance yourself."

Chapter 35

Tuesday, 2:30 p.m. in Paris

I retraced my steps until I reached Boulevard Saint-Michel, and from there I took the most direct route back to our hotel, which involved a series of side streets.

"One new message, Monsieur Martin, but I had a very hard time understanding the caller," the desk clerk said apologetically. "He was calling from the US."

"Really," I said, as he handed me the message. I thought that perhaps one of her sisters had called, but it was from a man named

"Jacque Handaler." I didn't know anyone named Jacque. And the area code was 312, which I knew to be from downtown Chicago. I just assumed the desk clerk had made a mistake.

When I reached the room, I immediately crossed off all the "Today" entries on my list. Ordinarily that gives me a sense of satisfaction. But this time it was different. As my ballpoint pen made a line through Love Lock, the last entry, I grew deeply saddened.

I turned off all the lights, pulled the thick drapes closed over the window, stacked up all four pillows on Jill's side of the bed, and just sat there staring at wallpaper that I could see only in my mind.

"How did life ever get to this point?" I said aloud. "How did it ever get this crazy? Why?"

All sorts of thoughts darted through my mind—not plans, just fragments, and random thoughts.

"Is Jill gone? Must I force myself to accept it? Will I never see her again? And now I learn that I might be dying. If I have to go back to the US without her, what will I tell her family? Is it possible that she left me? … No, that could not have happened. But if she were dead, why has nothing turned up? People do not just disappear, not even in Paris. But she did—somehow Jill apparently *did* disappear."

Chapter 36

Tuesday, 5:10 p.m. in Paris

P aul," Jill said. "Where are you?" But there was no one close enough to hear her.

She looked around and discovered that her left arm was strapped to a metal bed, and that there was an IV taped to it.

She tried to sit up, but when she did she felt a piercing pain in her head.

What is this? she wondered. *Is this a hospital? Could I be in a hospital?*

Mustering all her strength, she screamed, "Can anyone hear me?"

Again pain shot through her head, so she remained still, hoping it would subside.

Finally, a nurse looked into the room.

The nurse was a petite woman, with short brown hair held back by a pair of heavy-framed reading glasses, which she wore on top of her head.

She looked in, and upon seeing her patient was awake, she smiled.

"Bonsoir, Madame."

"Nurse, do you speak English?"

"Oui," she said tentatively, "but only a little."

"Is my fiancé here?"

"No, Madame. I don't think so. In fact I don't think you've had any visitors at all."

"Where am I?"

"Madame, this is Hospital Hotel-Dieu."

"So, this *is* a hospital. Why am I in a *hospital*? And how did I get here?"

"You have had a terrible accident. You bumped your head. It is *very* serious."

"Bumped my head? How did I do that?"

"A robber took your purse, and you fell down. Your head hit the ..." the nurse halted, searching for the right words. "Your head hit the ... walk ... the concrete."

"Where's Paul, my fiancé? And how long have I been here?"

The nurse picked up the chart and said, "It says you came in two days ago. You have slept the whole time. I should call the doctor and tell him you are awake."

The nurse started to leave the room to get the treating physician.

"Wait!" Jill shouted.

The nurse turned to her and replied, "I need to get your doctor, Madame Bertrand. I will tell …"

"What did you call me? Did you say, *Bertrand*? My name isn't Bertrand. My name is *Talbot*, Jill Talbot. And it's not Madame. I'm not married. And my fiancé is Paul Martin."

"I'm sorry, the sheet says you are Sylvia Bertrand. Could you be mistaken?"

"I know who I am. My name is Jill Talbot. Go, please, get the doctor."

Jill lay there silently, but her mind was racing. She discovered that if she did not stir or try to talk, the pain in her head became bearable.

After a few moments, the doctor who had been treating her hurried into the room with the nurse close behind.

"*Mademoiselle,*" he said. "My name is Dr. Jean Cartier. I'm the doctor who has been looking after you. How are you doing?"

The doctor appeared to be in his late sixties. Balding on top, he wore a green scrub with his name embroidered on the upper left side. Underneath it he had on a blue shirt and a white tie with the fleur-de-lis emblem scattered through the material. His eyes matched the blue of the shirt, and he spoke softly and with unaffected concern.

"I want to see Paul, my fiancé," Jill said.

"Mademoiselle, when they brought you in, you were alone. No fiancé. But we will see if we can find him. You say his name is Paul,

Paul Bertrand?"

"No! My fiancé's name is *Martin*, Paul Martin. And my name is Jill Talbot, not Bertrand. We're staying at a hotel in the Latin Quarter. We're from America."

"But we have you listed as Sylvia Bertrand, and that you reside right here in Paris. That was the name on your business cards. Your purse was stolen, so the only thing we had to make an identification were the business cards in your coat pocket."

"Sylvia Bertrand is an artist we met earlier … earlier Sunday, I think. She had just closed her gallery in Paris, in the Latin Quarter. She shut the doors for good and she was in the process of moving to the US."

Jill's head was splitting, so she laid it down on the pillow and remained silent for a moment.

"I had told her, Sylvia Bertrand, that I would contact her when we got back to the States, and we would see if we could help her in any way. That's why I had her cards in my pocket. She had her email address on her card."

"But we tried to call the number on the card, and no one answered."

"Exactly! No one could possibly answer her phone anymore—it's the number for her gallery. And it's now closed. Sunday was her last day in Paris. I suspect she is now already in the US. She *couldn't* answer her phone," Jill explained, trying to lie as still as possible to allay the pain.

"I will call the Police Nationale immediately," the doctor said, "and inform them of the mistake. It is *very* good to see you are awake. You gave us quite a scare. That was a terrible bump. For a time we thought we might have to operate to relieve the swelling;

it was causing pressure on your brain. But it responded to medication, and now you are fully awake. And that is a very good sign."

"Hotel California!" Jill lifted her head and cried out as loudly as possible, just before the doctor left the room.

"Yes?" Dr. Cartier said.

"I just remembered. We are staying at the Hotel California. Over by the Sorbonne."

"Really? That's not far from here. I will let the investigator know that."

"Wait!" Jill shouted, again stopping the doctor before he could leave.

"Yes?"

"Our hotel is not far from here? Is that what you said? Where, exactly is this hospital?"

"Mademoiselle, if you lean forward and look out of your window, what do you see?"

Jill pushed herself up to her elbows and painfully forced her eyes to focus on a nearby building.

"Is that Notre Dame?"

"Yes, indeed it is. You were injured right outside the doors of the cathedral, and now you are healing just meters away."

Chapter 37

Tuesday, 12:05 p.m. on Sugar Island

So far all had progressed as planned. Griffon's Funeral Home had taken care of all the arrangements. They delivered Reg's body to the airline. Stein's Funeral Services in Brooklyn would pick up the body from LaGuardia and deliver it to the Calvary Cemetery for the ten a.m. graveside service.

Griffon's had assured Jack that there remained nothing for him to worry about with regard to his friend's funeral—it would all be handled professionally. Jack had a high level of confidence in

Griffon's, and so he was secure in releasing the responsibility into their hands. His faith was justified.

Even though Chippewa International Airport was small by any standard, Jack still made sure he arrived with time to spare. With only one set of connections to New York each day, he could not afford to make a mistake.

No sooner had he settled into his preferred-class seat, than a familiar voice requested his help.

"Jack, would you please give me a hand with this? It's a bit heavy for me."

Jack was in shock. Standing beside him in the aisle was former First Lady Allison Fulbright. She was disguised as Bernadette Lowery—the persona she had developed while living in New York in order to afford herself freedom to move about without Secret Service attention.

Her disguised appearance was not substantially different from what he'd remembered. She had, however, lost some weight. Wisely he did not comment about that. For one thing, he had heard that she was in recovery from a bout with cancer. And second, it's never appropriate to comment on a lady's weight.

"Oh my God! Allison … Bernadette. You're looking fantastic. But what are you doing here?"

"Well, after you help me put this bag in the overhead, I'll tell you."

A million thoughts raced through Jack's mind as he stood up beside her and lifted the heavy, soft-sided briefcase to the compartment above his seat.

"What in the world are you carrying around with you?" Jack asked. "It feels like a small automobile engine."

"The *case* weighs only four pounds, but the contents weigh twenty-two," she replied.

Jack's mind was racing. He recalled the original members of the assassination plot: James, Jerry, Reg, and Steve. And they were all dead—Allison and he were the lone survivors.

What in the hell could she be doing here, he wondered, *at this time, in disguise, on my plane?*

Once both Jack and Allison had settled into their seats, Allison began to talk.

"Let me clear the air on this one thing first," she said. "I know you must be convinced that I had something to do with your friend's unfortunate accident. Well, Jack, I did not. I hope you can take my word on that."

"That's interesting," Jack said. "Then who did?"

"Don't know. I have a theory, but I don't know anything for sure."

"Tell me what you do know," Jack commanded.

"It's a long story—" Allison started to say when Jack interrupted.

"We've got an hour and twenty minutes before we land in Detroit," he said. "Why don't you tell me what you do know?"

Chapter 38

Tuesday, 1:05 p.m. on Sugar Island

I will make it as short as possible," she said. "As you know, I had paid Reg a lot of money to do a favor for me. And he never fulfilled his end.

"I wanted to get my gold back, but I did not have any idea where he had hidden it. He then faked his death, which made it even more difficult.

"When questions arose regarding whether he had actually died, I began to suspect that he might have had it buried in or beneath his coffin at Calvary Cemetery. That's when I moved forward on having his body exhumed.

"But when some of the gold turned up in Florida, I suspected that not all of it was hidden. Apparently he needed some of it for living expenses."

"And you had recorded the DNA signatures from each of the pieces," Jack said. "Isn't that right?"

"Exactly. I knew they'd be too unique to sell intact—that whoever held them would melt them down, eventually. So I just put the word out. And when some of it showed up in Ft. Lauderdale, I sent a team down there immediately."

"To kill Reg?" Jack asked.

"No. That would have accomplished nothing," Allison stated. "I was after what was rightfully mine. I was angry, but I cared nothing about revenge. Reg would have been useless to me dead."

"Go on," Jack commanded.

"My guys acquired the surveillance video from the place that purchased the gold, and it showed someone with a beard, but who otherwise looked a lot like Reg, accepting payment for nearly a pound of my gold.

"My investigators located Reg in the Ft. Lauderdale area and have been monitoring his movements.

"Once he made contact with you, and I suspected he was about to, I knew it would only be a matter of time before he tried to meet with you. That's when I sent another team up to the Soo to watch for him."

"And they, your people in the Soo, they had nothing to do with

Reg's death?" Jack asked.

"Absolutely nothing," Allison said. "They were under very strict orders, and those orders did not involve killing anyone."

For a moment, Jack considered asking her about the killing of the two lawyers on the Sugar Island Ferry but decided against it.

"You said you had a theory?" Jack asked.

"More like a guess," Allison said. "I'll tell you what I think about it. My guys were going to pick him up at his hotel the morning after he got into town. I'm sure they would have roughed him up a bit, but nothing serious. My thinking was that once he realized that we were on to him, he would give up the gold. Especially if he thought it could put Pam in a bad situation."

"I'd agree with that," Jack said. "Reg would not hold back anything if he thought his wife could be in danger."

"That's precisely what I thought," she agreed. "But when we went after him, we found that an ambulance had already beat us to it."

"So then who killed him?" Jack asked.

"My bet is that someone followed him up here from Florida— someone who discovered that he was selling gold that had been melted down into non-traditional ingots. I think it might have had something to do with the shop that bought the gold from him. They shocked us when they gave up the surveillance video with little resistance. Hard to know. I just know that whoever it was, they didn't know where the gold was hidden, so they were not of interest to me."

"Why would they kill him?" Jack asked.

"An accident, I'd guess. They were probably unprofessional— trying to coerce something out of him and got a little too rough.

And maybe he had a heart attack."

"That makes sense. They could have injected him with heroin to loosen him up—I doubt they ever intended to kill him."

"In Reg's mind, just the thought of having heroin in his body might have been enough to kill him," Allison suggested. "Reg was such a health nut. He'd do anything to avoid having a needle stuck in him. If they were injecting *anything* into his body, he just might give up the gold—"

"Or give up the ghost," Jack finished her sentence. "I think he actually did have a heart attack. He could not handle the notion of drugs in his body."

"I knew you would have suspected that I had him killed," Allison said. "I'm glad we got that ironed out."

"But that's not the reason you're on this plane with me," Jack said. "You've got something else on your mind."

Jack was sure Allison was telling him the truth about Reg. For one thing, she was totally aware that to kill Reg would require the killing of Jack as well. And she was not ready to do that.

At the same time Jack was equally certain that Allison was behind the killing of the two lawyers on the Sugar Island Ferry and was most likely the client who hired the Crofts to kill Steve, one of the original conspirators. But he did not care to hear Allison confess to those hits. In neither case was Jack personally attached to the victims, and Allison knew that.

"You're right," Allison replied. "I'm here because I think we can help one another—just like old times."

Allison couched her proposition in such a fashion in order to remind Jack just how intertwined their lives had been back when she was the first lady and her husband was president. During those eight years, Jack was their number-one go-to guy. If something—anything—needed to get done, and if the tactics to be employed were unsavory, Jack was the one they called on.

She believed that if she could get Jack on board with her one more time, he would be hugely useful to her once she was elected.

"Jack," she said. "I want to get my gold back. I'm sure you don't know where Reg hid it, but I'm sure if there is one person in the world who can find it, you can."

"What makes you think I could possibly be interested in helping you with this?" Jack asked. "Reg was my good friend, probably my best friend. Even though he's dead, why would I want to go against his wishes?"

"Because his wishes would include the well-being of his widow—her financial well-being. And I can help with that."

"What are you suggesting?" Jack asked.

"That bag you stashed for me earlier," Allison said. "That bag contains twenty-two pounds of brand new one-hundred dollar bills."

"A million dollars," Jack said.

"Exactly right," Allison said with a smile. "One million with no strings. Whether or not you agree to go after the gold, that money is yours. But, if you find the gold, Reg's widow will receive five million dollars, and you will also receive five million. That should just about set her up for the rest of her life—she's a pretty simple woman."

Jack leaned back and thought about what she had just said to him. While he did not like Allison Fulbright, he knew her to be good on her promises, at least this promise. He knew that both of the Fulbrights subscribed to the unwritten law that you never screwed your hit man. If she promised to pay Pam five million, she would be good for it.

"What if I don't locate all the gold?" Jack asked. "What then?"

"I've considered that," she replied. "I know that Reg has already disposed of some of it. So, if you can locate a substantial portion of it, I will see that both you and Pam receive five percent."

Jack thought for a few more moments and then spoke.

"No matter how much of it I find, Pam is to receive the first ten million. I don't want anything aside from the money in your carry-on. That will finance my efforts. If I find the whole one hundred million dollars' worth, she gets ten million. But if I find only ten million, she gets it all. And there will be no time limits, none. And you will *not* engage anyone else in this effort. Period."

Allison did not have to think about it.

"Done," she responded.

"Then I don't think we have anything else to talk about," Jack said, standing to remove the briefcase from above their heads.

He then feigned a quick smile and retired to an empty seat toward the rear of the plane. He sat down and closed his eyes.

Allison sat back in her seat. She was as happy to be rid of Jack as he was to move away from her. The deal had been struck in such a way that all parties were satisfied.

But more important to Allison than anything else, even more than the prospect of Jack's finding the gold and returning it to her, was the revelation that Jack accepted the fact that she had nothing to do with Reg's death. She knew that if Jack blamed her for his friend's death, her days on earth would end abruptly.

Allison smiled.

Chapter 39

Tuesday, 3:03 p.m. in Detroit

The next thing Jack realized was when the pilot engaged the landing gear on the glide path just south of Detroit Metropolitan Airport. Seconds later the wheels screeched on the runway and the plane began to slow down.

Jack had slept for the last part of the trip—with twenty-two pounds of crisp one-hundred dollar bills resting on his lap.

"Sure hope Allison is long gone before I get off," he moaned. "Don't want to deal with her anymore today. Or anymore at *any* time."

He looked at his watch as he stood to deplane. "Three-fifteen," he muttered.

Everyone on the plane was standing, either in the aisle or at their seats. Jack sensed a cool waft of air against his face. He knew that signaled that the door had been opened for the passengers to get off.

Without realizing it, he found himself staring in the direction of Allison's seat. Just as the passengers began making their way onto the jet bridge, Allison leaned over the aisle seat and looked back toward Jack.

Their eyes met. She affected an impersonal smile and waved. Jack smiled. She then turned and walked onto the covered walkway.

Why did I even look in her direction? Jack asked himself.

It would have been so much nicer for him had he not seen her face that last time.

Chapter 40

Tuesday, 10:00 p.m. in Paris

Jill asked her nurse if she could have the doctor come back to her room. But the nurse told her that the doctor was off for the night.

"He will be back tomorrow—Wednesday. He will see you then."

"Did he call my hotel? Did he talk to my fiancé?" she asked.

"The doctor called the Police Nationale and left a message for the investigator … he told the investigator that you had emerged from your coma. The investigator is off until tomorrow at five p.m. He's on holiday."

"Oh my God! When … *how* do I get out of here?" Jill asked.

"That's up to the doctor and the police. They want to talk to you about the robbery. And I think the hospital wants to know about your insurance. Anyway, nothing can happen until tomorrow. The investigator handling your case, that is Monsieur Mickael Pouliquen, will not be in until five p.m. tomorrow."

The nurse held up an open hand indicating five p.m., as though Jill did not understand.

"Can you at least let me make a phone call?" Jill requested.

"I'm sorry, Mademoiselle. The doctor said that you would have to clear that with the Police Nationale, and that can't happen until the investigator gets back. I'm sorry, truly sorry."

Chapter 41

Tuesday, 4:10 p.m. in Detroit

Jack was very pleased that he did not run into or even see Allison again—not after that parting glance just before she deplaned in Detroit.

He had been concerned that she would be waiting for him in

the Detroit terminal. After all, she did know that he would have over an hour to kill before boarding his connection to New York.

Jack did not spend a lot of time looking for her during his stopover. Once off the plane at DTW, Jack hurried through the McNamara Terminal until he found an acceptable coffee shop. There he picked up a *Detroit Free Press* from an empty table and hid behind it, sipping his coffee.

As he sat there thinking, Jack found himself unexpectedly content with his meeting with Allison. In short order, they had covered all the important points.

The matter of the gold was determined—he would find it, and Pam would be set for life.

She had told him that she did not have Reg killed, and that while she had a theory, she did not have any concrete knowledge as to who did kill Reg. Jack believed her.

Jack did not want to hear her confess that she was responsible for Steve's death. He knew that it was her work—just as was the killing of the two lawyers on the Sugar Island Ferry. Jack knew that had he asked her about those killings, she would have told him the truth. But that was information he did not need, nor did he want it.

He did wonder why she was so eager to get her hands on the gold, so much so that she was willing to give up a sizable percentage of it as a finder's fee.

Jack could think of only two reasons for this degree of earnestness.

One, she might need it to finance a run for the White House. While on the surface that notion might seem feasible, he knew that she had control over several hundred million dollars in cash.

It was partly in the form of personal wealth, with a sizable portion of it being offered by a family friend and a notorious financier.

Jack didn't think that she would really need that gold to fund her campaign.

In Jack's opinion, the only other reason for her passionate desire to get her hands on that gold right now most likely would be so she could use it to finance some very expensive clandestine effort—such as another attempt at assassinating the president.

Lending weight to that theory was her recent murder of Steve. With that hit, there remained only him with direct knowledge of the failed attempt.

Jack had always viewed Steve as a loose end—no reason to think Allison did not share that concern. So Jack sensed relief with Steve's death.

However, the fact that he and Allison were the only surviving members of the original conspiracy concerned Jack considerably.

For the time being he served a purpose in the overall plan—he would eventually find her gold. But once that job was completed, he then intended to keep a safe distance from the Fulbrights—if there ever could be such a thing as a safe distance.

Jack remained in the coffee shop until it was time to board the plane to New York.

Chapter 42

Tuesday, 7:30 p.m. in New York

On arrival at LaGuardia, Jack switched on his phone. Immediately he saw that he had a text message from Kate.

With twenty-two pounds of crispy Franklins hanging from his

left arm, and his own carry-on from his right, he delayed reading Kate's text until he had found an appropriate seat at the gate just inside the terminal.

Slipping on his reading glasses, he opened it.

"Dad. Still planning to meet at bar. Hope tht's ok."

That arrangement was just fine with Jack. While it would have felt good to see a friendly face at the airport, Jack had to make certain that the airline, or Stein's Funeral Services, did not mishandle Reg's body.

He had taken every precaution available to him before leaving the Soo. He made sure that he physically observed the casket as it was dropped off at Chippewa International Airport by Griffon's Funeral Home. But he had no direct knowledge that it had been properly transferred in Detroit.

Nor did he have direct access to observe that the casket was picked up by Stein's. But he did have a twenty-four-hour number for Stein's.

So he remained seated at the gate until he received visual confirmation that the New York funeral home had actually received the body and had loaded it onto a transport vehicle.

The whole issue with Reg posed a tedious task for Jack. He spent nearly two hours seated at the gate—during much of which he was in direct communication with Stein's employees. He knew better than to assume the transfer had occurred until the driver confirmed that the body was off airport property and was in transit.

As soon as Jack was convinced that there was no one left that he could harass, he made a shot for the taxi line. He seldom checked in any luggage, so he did not have to worry about that delay.

"Kate. Are you at the hotel yet?" Jack asked as he settled back and stretched out his legs in his Ford Escape Hybrid taxi.

"Just walking in," she replied. "Are you already here?"

"No. I'm in a taxi. Just leaving LaGuardia. I stuck around until I was sure Stein's had taken care of Reg. I should be at the hotel in half an hour. Traffic shouldn't be bad."

"I just heard that there is an accident on the Kennedy coming into the city," Kate said. "It's really slow. I think you'd do better to take the Midtown Tunnel."

"That's what my driver said," Jack replied.

"Hey, I've got some good news about tomorrow."

"What's that?" Jack asked.

"I have to take a trip upstate tomorrow. To question a potential witness in my case, the one I discussed with you. The department made arrangements for me to fly out of LaGuardia in the afternoon. So I can drive you to the airport, park, and see you off. How cool is that?"

"I thought you had a prelim coming up?" Jack asked.

"Prosecutor put it off for a day. I thought you would like some company while you wait," Kate said with a sly smile.

"That's great," Jack said. "Where are you flying to?"

"Albany. I catch a shuttle ninety minutes after your flight."

Chapter 43

Wednesday, 10:00 a.m. in Paris

I didn't move from the bed until late the next morning. I don't recall sleeping, but part of my thinking must have been a dream, so I suppose that I did sleep.

Usually, I would watch the news and have a glass of milk with cookies before going to bed. Last night I didn't even have milk. I simply propped myself up with pillows on Jill's bed and waited in the dark for morning. I didn't care if I slept or not. I knew that I wouldn't die from sleep deprivation—if I grew sufficiently weary, I would eventually drift off.

A casual glance at the bed suggested a single queen-sized unit. However, removing the spread revealed two very narrow beds that were simply pushed together. Jill and I had joked that we should have brought with us a couple zip ties to hook the beds together.

When I woke up, the room was totally dark—not because the sun had not yet risen, but because I had the drapes so tightly closed.

And I was no longer sitting on Jill's bed. Somehow during the night I must have tossed the pillows onto the floor and crawled beneath the cover.

I looked at my computer and discovered that it was ten a.m.

"That's late," I said. "I must have slept."

Having a list took some of the pressure off. Again, all I had to do was follow the charted course and cross off the landmarks.

The first thing I did was to call the front desk to ask for messages. There were none. I crossed off "Front Desk."

Next, I logged onto my email account. I had emails from all three of Jill's siblings. It was killing me to have to give them the bad news—that there was no word yet on their sister. But I had to do it.

As always, I kept it short: "Hi guys—Sorry but there is no news yet. I will contact the Police Nationale again today, along with the US Embassy. I do that every day. I will then go to Notre Dame and talk to employees. I have been doing that every day as well. I have also been making handouts with your sister's picture on it. I will take some more down there, but I think they are getting sick of seeing my face—that's too bad, but I'm going to do it anyway. I will contact you as soon as I find out anything. –Paul."

And then there was an email from someone named Jack Handler. I remembered the fractured message I had received at the front desk and concluded that *Jacque Handaler* was actually Jack Handler. But I still didn't recognize the name.

"Mr. Martin," the message read. "My name is Jack Handler. I am a private investigator licensed in Illinois. Lesley Wallace, whom I believe to be your fiancée's older sister, asked me to look into your situation. I understand that at some point on last Sunday Jill went missing—that she walked off to help a lost child during Mass at Notre Dame and that she has not yet been found. I did talk to her other sister as well. They have informed me just how appreciative they are for your communications with them. They also told me that you have engaged the Police Nationale, as well as the US Embassy. Those were the correct steps in a situation such as this. I would like you to give me a call at 302-555-1686 ASAP. That is my cell phone. I have it with me at all times. So you should dial 00-1-302-555-1686. That would put you directly through to my cell. I look forward to talking to you about this most distressing matter."

"That would be just fine," I grumbled out loud, "if I only had a cell phone."

I had already attempted to call using the phone in the room and the one in the front lobby, but with no success. I'm not sure why.

So I opted to send Mr. Handler an email.

Chapter 44

Wednesday, 11:00 a.m. in Paris

Jill was beginning to feel like a prisoner. She waited impatiently for her doctor to see her. She was, however, pleased that her head no longer throbbed.

Finally, just after eleven a.m., Dr. Cartier came through the door.

"Mademoiselle Talbot," he said. "You are looking very well today. You've got color in your face. Your eyes are brighter. Tell me, how do you feel?"

"The nurse told me that you did not call my hotel—is that right?"

"I called the investigator in charge of your case. I was following the orders he gave me—"

"But he's not in. So you didn't actually call him, did you?"

"That's right. I left a message. He was on holiday. He will be in today at five p.m. I will call him again then. But he might already have the message. I was told that often the investigators will call in for messages on their days off. He might even be on his way here this very minute."

"Then will you at least let me call my fiancé? He has to be worried sick."

"I'm so sorry, Mademoiselle Talbot. But I have to do what the authorities told me to do. *He* needs to talk to you first, and he will be out until five p.m. today."

"Then, if I don't hear from him by six p.m., will you let me call my fiancé?"

"We will have to wait for him to call or come to the hospital. Only he can make that decision."

"Isn't there someone else in his office who can help me?"

"It doesn't work like that. He's the investigator in charge of your case—he has to be the one who makes those decisions."

Chapter 45

Wednesday, 2:00 p.m. in Paris

B y two p.m. I was able to cross off most of the tasks on my list. All that remained were packing and Love Lock. This time I even stopped by the Police Nationale to visit the investigator. I read my phonetic spelling of his name to the officer on duty, but she could not understand me. I then showed her his card. She smiled as she told me to have a seat, and then she called him. I think her smile was more a reaction to my having butchered his name than any effort to be friendly.

Nevertheless, about a minute later he walked up to where I was sitting.

"Bonjour, Monsieur Martin. Thank you for stopping by. I hope you have good news for me. Have you heard from your fiancée?"

My heart sank, even though the news he gave me was exactly what I expected. I then asked him what I should do about my flight tomorrow morning if Jill still had not returned.

He said that I should do whatever I had to do, but leaving Paris was not to be one of my options. He was *very* firm about that. I even got the feeling that he was ready to lock me up were he to suspect that I might be planning to leave.

I assured him that I had already talked to my embassy, and they told me to make arrangements with my hotel should my stay need to be extended. He seemed willing to accept that.

By the time I left I was almost regretting that I had shown up in person. In fact, every single encounter with the investigator left me feeling worse off afterward. I was sure, however, that I had done the right thing. His reaction to my question about leaving convinced me that he would have had me picked up should he have considered me a flight risk.

As I walked out of Police Nationale, I had to wait for an ambulance dropping off an emergency case directly across the street, at Hospital Hotel-Dieu.

Chapter 46

Wednesday, 9:00 a.m. in New York

J ack," Roger said. "How are you planning to get to the cemetery?"

"I had planned on catching a taxi. How about you?"

"I'm out front right now. Can I give you a lift?"

"Yeah. Certainly," Jack said. "I was just about to check out. I'll be right down."

Jack was running a little late—uncomfortably late. He had

spent the past fifteen minutes on the phone with Lesley Wallace discussing the latest news about her missing sister.

Jack had explained to her that immediately after the funeral today he would head to the airport to catch a flight to Paris.

Lesley told him that Paul and her sister were due to fly home on Thursday morning, but that Paul was not going to leave France until he had located Jill.

By the way Lesley explained it to Jack, it was Paul who had made the decision to remain in France unless her sister were found, but Jack knew that the decision as to whether he stayed in Paris was not Paul's to make.

Were Jill not to turn up alive and in good condition before the scheduled trip back to the US, the Police Nationale would block him from traveling. Not only was Paul a person of interest in the eyes of French authority, but he was the prime suspect.

That, of course, was not how Lesley saw it. In her eyes Paul was every bit as much a victim in the situation as was her sister.

And that's exactly how Jack wanted her to feel. If matters turned totally south at some time in the future, there would be plenty of finger-pointing taking place. But for the short term, it would be best for the whole family to work together in trust and unity.

Jack scooped up his two bags and headed toward the elevator.

He had wanted to talk to Roger face to face while in New York but was beginning to think it wouldn't happen on this trip. The drive from the hotel to the cemetery would now give him the chance he wanted.

However, just as Jack approached the revolving doors at the main entry, a voice from the past blasted across the lobby.

"Handler!"

Jack stopped and turned around. It was Captain Spencer, Kate's boss.

"Spencer," Jack said. It had taken him a couple seconds to determine who was barking out his name.

"*Captain* Spencer. What are you doing here?"

Chapter 47

Wednesday, 9:18 a.m. in New York

K ate informed me that you were in town to attend a funeral, and I wanted to talk to you," Captain Spencer said.

Jack glanced down at his watch and then back up at the captain. He was carefully weighing his next words when the captain spoke.

"I know it's rather late. But if you'll spare me just a couple minutes. I'll be brief."

Jack liked Captain Spencer. And he knew how important it could be to Kate's career for him to treat her boss with the utmost respect. So he smiled and said, "Captain, it's great to see you. Of course, I've got some time to talk to you. What's on your mind?"

Captain Spencer led Jack over to a quiet spot in the lobby, and they sat down on two overstuffed brown leather chairs. Jack placed his cases on the floor between them.

"Jack," Captain Spencer said, "do you know anything about the case Kate is currently working?"

"No," Jack replied.

Even though that was not an entirely forthright response to the captain's question, it was the only one Jack was comfortable with.

Had he given Kate's boss reason to think that she had been discussing an ongoing investigation with anyone outside the department, it could be troublesome to her.

Best to let the captain tell me what he wants me to hear, Jack reasoned.

"Well, Jack, this is a big sticky case. I can't tell you very much about it. And Kate should not talk to you at all regarding any of the details."

Jack was growing impatient. "Captain, if neither you nor Kate can discuss this with me, what are we doing here *not* talking about it? I have to bury my friend. Maybe we can do this at a later time?"

"Keep your pants on, Jack," the captain said. "There's some shit that's come up regarding it. Kate doesn't know about it yet. But it involves you directly. I'm here as a courtesy to you, as Kate's father, to give you a heads-up. I have no doubt that you are going to get served with a grand jury subpoena. I thought I'd give you a chance to think about it, and maybe you could tell me what you know, and maybe I can discourage your getting called in to testify."

"What are you saying?" Jack asked. The captain now had his full attention.

"This guy that got whacked, allegedly by the killer that Kate caught. This Croft guy. Well, the fellow that Croft killed was named Steve Williams. And it now appears that Mr. Steve Williams was somewhat expecting to get killed. So much so that he left a letter with his uncle, who happens to be a DC attorney. His instructions that accompanied the letter stated that it should be turned over to the US Attorney General himself, should Mr. Williams ever meet a violent death—namely, should he ever be murdered."

"And how does that involve me?" Jack asked.

"I just received a copy of that letter from the Justice Department," Captain Spencer said. "Almost every line of that letter was redacted by the time it got to me. About the only parts of it that weren't blacked out were your name, which appeared twice, and the name of Reginald Black. His name appeared half a dozen times."

"Captain, I can assure you that I had nothing to do with this man's death. I met him on one occasion, and one occasion only. And Reg was there. Actually, he was with Reg. And now Reg is dead. So there's nothing more I can tell you about it. I certainly had nothing to do with this man's death, and neither did Reg. That's about it. What sort of a case are you building against this

Croft guy? Does the prosecutor think he's got enough to bring it to trial?"

"*She*, Jack, the prosecutor in this case is a female—Amanda Crow. That's her name. And she's very good friends with your daughter. In fact, the two of them are flying upstate later today to question a witness and take a deposition, in preparation for the grand jury. We don't know yet if we are going to have enough to prosecute. But I'm going to turn this letter over to Ms. Crow when they get back, and I would assume that she will discuss this with your daughter, and maybe that might be an issue for you. What do you think?"

"I'm hitching a ride with Kate to LaGuardia after the funeral. I assume that the prosecutor, Ms. Crow, will be with her. Should I mention to them that you questioned me about this?"

"That would be the thing to do, I would think. No point springing it on them blindly. Now, what can you tell me about this Steve Williams fellow?"

"Not much," Jack replied. "Reg knew him; I didn't. I think he, Mr. Williams, was in public relations. I can tell you that I didn't like what I saw. He had a mouth on him—the kind that made enemies. I think you might want to talk to the uncle. Had he read the letter before he delivered it to the Feds?"

"Says he never read it. I believed him."

"Believed? Past tense?"

Chapter 48

Wednesday, 9:29 a.m. in New York

Right," Captain Spencer replied. "He had a heart attack last evening while he was watching a game on TV. He died right there in his leather recliner."

"Wonderful," Jack said.

"Exactly what I thought."

"Any chance you can get your hands on the original document?" Jack asked.

"What do you think, Handler? You worked in DC more than I have. In fact, I think you knew the former president, President

Fulbright. Weren't you sort of his right-hand man?"

"No, that wasn't the case at all," Jack said. "He used me to vet some of his appointments. But that was the extent of it. I never worked for his office after his first term."

"As I understand it," the captain said, "this Steve Williams worked quite closely with the president during the second term. He served as a media/public relations advisor. Are you sure you didn't run into him back then?"

"Positive," Jack replied. "I recall seeing him one time, a year or so ago, and he was with Reg. We really didn't discuss anything of substance. I just recall him being someone I could do without seeing again. I didn't like him. What does Croft have to say about him? Can you put the two of them together?"

"Are you kidding?" Captain Spencer said. "He denies everything. But I really can't discuss this with you. I'll let you go now. I think you've got a car waiting for you out front. It's clogging everything up. But I suppose that's okay; it's got government plates. I'll see you around, Jack."

"Captain. It was good to see you," Jack said with a sincere smile as he turned to leave the hotel.

Given a choice, Jack always opted for the standard swinging doors—his lack of patience did not allow him to use slow-moving revolving doors.

Even before his hand touched the decorative push plate, he had already spotted Roger's vehicle. And just as Captain Spencer had suggested, it was obstructing the free flow of guests trying to check in.

After the Fed bailed out General Motors, most government agencies ordered massive numbers of Tahoes. But in 2013 the Secret Service leased twenty-three Fords, four of which were seven-passenger Explorer XLTs. Roger was driving one of them.

Jack could not see his friend through the tinted front windshield (which was prohibited for standard-use vehicles), but he knew it had to be Roger.

The ding-less Tuxedo Black Metallic looked as though it had just been driven out of a showroom. The side glass sported an even deeper tint. Of course, Roger had engaged the four-ways.

Out of the corner of his eye, Jack spotted a blue-on-white NYPD patrol car slowing to get a closer look at the Explorer because it was stopped too close to the building, a fire code violation. But when they realized it was a federal vehicle, they smirked and moved on.

"Jack, good to see you," Roger said, sounding a short blast on a siren to clear the taxi that was partially blocking his exit.

"Well, do you think we can bury our old buddy for good this time?" Roger continued.

Jack did not respond. He was still miffed that Roger had collaborated with Reg in the faking of his death.

After a few moments of silence, Jack asked, "Got any ideas who did it?"

"Not really," Roger responded. "But I have heard that some guys out of Florida have been talking. Shouldn't be too difficult for a good detective to get to the bottom of it, if he had a mind to."

"I suppose you know about Allison's offer?"

"Not much more than you and I discussed earlier. She did ask me if I thought that you would be willing to meet with her. She even suggested that I be present. I told her that I wanted to opt out of the meeting, simply because my role dictated that I should not participate. I did tell her that I believed you would be willing to discuss matters with her, but that she should arrange the meeting—not I. As I understand it, she wanted you to round up what's left of the gold Reg had received from her. If that's what you're talking about."

"She and I did speak briefly, and she offered me what amounts to a ten percent finder's fee," Jack said. "And probably a little more than that. Any idea what she has in mind? Why, all of a sudden, she has such a keen interest in retrieving that gold?"

"No, and I don't want to know either. Some things are just best left alone. And I suspect that might be one of them. Are you going to take her offer?"

Jack always regarded Roger highly. He would never intentionally mislead him or even hold back information. While it was true that Roger had helped Reg fake his death, and then subsequently withheld from Jack what he knew regarding Reg, Jack still had the utmost trust in his friend.

"I accepted her offer, but with some modifications," Jack answered. "I took some walking-around money upfront. And when I retrieve the gold for her, Pam is to receive ten million in cash. Those were my terms, and she accepted."

"Sounds reasonable," Roger said. "In fact, it sounds exactly the way Reg would have wanted it. He was very concerned about Pam's welfare, and he would have helped her more had he been able. But he knew that to sell some of the gold, in order to send her money, would have put her in jeopardy. Look what happened when he tried to get rid of even that small amount—it got him killed."

"From the way Allison described it," Jack said. "Some bad guys followed Reg from Florida when he came up to see me, and tried to squeeze information out of him—where the rest of the gold was. And they accidently killed him."

"Are you going after them?" Roger asked.

"I'm going after the gold. It's not improbable that in doing that, I just might run into them. But finding Reg's killers is not on the top of my agenda, at least not yet."

"I'll see if I can come up with something with regard to who his killers might be. I'd sure like to see them pay for it, but not in a courtroom. Too many things go wrong when lawyers get involved."

"I know what you mean," Jack agreed. "But about that gold. You were around when Reg went into hiding. Do you have any idea where he might have stashed it?"

"None," Roger said without hesitation. "But you know, he was adamant about you having his clothes. Do you recall? We dropped them off for you?"

"Right," Jack replied. "They were a mess ... all that blood. He must have almost bled out. I don't think I've seen that much blood leak out of a *survivor*."

"He did lose a lot of blood," Roger agreed. "But once they stopped it and got him sewed up, he really healed fast. No vital organs were even scratched. And you know, Reg was in great physical condition. We pulled him out of that hospital the same night he went in, and moved him under the care of a private physician. Within a couple days he was out and about. But he insisted that you receive his clothing."

"He had a reason, I'm sure," Jack said.

"Do you know what that might be?"

"He left a puzzle in his pants," Jack said. "It was soaked in blood but still readable."

"Really? An honest-to-God *puzzle*? Did it come with a decoder ring? You know, like they used to put in your dad's Cracker Jack box. Did you ever try to solve it?"

"No. Not yet," Jack replied. "But I probably will now that I've accepted Allison's offer. You probably know that she also has a copy of it. Must be she couldn't do anything with it, or she wouldn't have called me in."

Traffic was heavy on the FDR along the East River. The sun had broken through momentarily, which made an otherwise gloomy light-raincoat day a bit more bearable. After Roger jumped over to the entrance to the Midtown Tunnel, it was a quick trip from there, under the East River and then directly along 495 to the entrance of Calvary Cemetery in Queens.

Of course, their actual drive time was shortened by Roger's liberal application of flashers and sirens.

"Is that what she was after? The night she broke into your apartment in New York?"

Roger recalled that two of Allison's men gained entry into Jack's apartment while he was sleeping, immediately after Reg had been shot. But Roger did not know what they were after—or even if they had actually taken anything from the room.

"Exactly," Jack said. "It was the night after we had freed Kate from her abductors. I had taken a knock on the head, and both Reg and Kate were wounded. By the time I got back to the apartment, I was so whipped I almost blacked out. While I was sleeping, someone came in with a key, and that's all they took—the puzzle. And Reg's blood-stained clothes."

"Maybe I'm missing something," Roger chuckled, "but why would he do a puzzle? Why not some sort of digital encryption? Isn't a puzzle just a little simplistic?"

"Maybe," Jack said. "But a good cryptogram is virtually impossible to decipher without the key. That is, if you keep it short. If you can limit the number of characters to under twenty, no computer program can crack it without the key."

"Do you have the key for Reg's puzzle?"

"That's probably the problem Allison's people ran into. Reg didn't provide the key. She doesn't have it, and I don't think I have it either."

"So what good is the puzzle then?"

"Maybe I'll get lucky," Jack said. "Or maybe Reg gave me the key and I just haven't recognized it yet. Actually, I haven't given this puzzle one minute of thought to this point. Maybe after I get back from Paris I'll be able to find some serious time to apply to it."

"Paris?" Roger asked in disbelief. "What the hell. Are you kidding me? Are you actually going to go to Paris and track down that poor fellow's runaway bride? Don't they have the Police Nationale for that anymore?"

"I know what you're saying," Jack agreed. "But you and I both know that the authorities are not going to invest a lot of resources tracking down some missing American girl without something to go on besides her boyfriend's story—at least not right away. And it's already been longer than we like. She's now been missing well over seventy-two hours. And the missing girl is my neighbor. She's a Sugar Island Girl."

"How old is this girl? Isn't she like twenty years old?"

"She's twenty-two," Jack replied. "But that's not the point. She's a true Sugar Island Girl. She's strong-minded and very resourceful. I have to agree with her sisters. Something serious is amiss over there. They are totally convinced that her boyfriend had nothing to do with it."

"And he's the one the Police Nationale like for it?" Roger asked. "Isn't that right?"

"Paul, the boyfriend didn't come out and say that specifically, but that's the standard unwritten law—to make the husband or, in this case, the boyfriend, prove his innocence. And without a body, or proof that the female actually met with some sort of foul play … that is, she didn't just run off with some French lad with a fancy leather jacket, then they're going to view him as their prime suspect. I'm thinking I might be able to shake things up a bit."

"Get yourself arrested, if you're not careful," Roger warned. "Better not pull any crap over there, because I can't help you, and our State Department might not want to help you."

"I'm just thinking, they're professional law enforcement. If I show up and rattle some cages, maybe I can help the kids out. I'm really hoping it's just some sort of argument. Or that she did hook up with a guy. We don't know anything about their relationship. … There's just a ton of unknowns here. About all I know for sure is that this girl is my neighbor on Sugar Island, and her sister is one of Red's teachers. Actually, Lesley is Red's *favorite* teacher. I've got to give it my best shot."

"I hear you," Roger said. "You can count on my help, for whatever it's worth."

"I do need your help." Jack quickly accepted his offer.

Chapter 49

Wednesday, 10:04 a.m. in New York

This case I'm tossing in the back of your vehicle, it contains one million dollars. Obviously I can't stick it in a bank, and I don't want to mess with safety deposit boxes. I would like you to take care of it for me. Will you do that?"

"Sure."

"If anything should happen to me, I'd like you to see that Pam gets half and Kate gets half."

"I can arrange that," Roger agreed.

"And you can keep the case for yourself," Jack chuckled. "I think it's a pretty good one. After all, it used to belong to Allison. And she never buys junk."

"Thanks, I'll certainly treasure it," Roger said. "Perhaps I should store your ashes in it. You know, in case something were to happen to you."

"What makes you think I would opt for cremation?" Jack chuckled. "But if I did, how is it you think you'd end up with the remains?"

"Jack, o' buddy, no one you know will want to pay for your funeral. You'll meet your end in the furnace. And as far as your ashes are concerned, I'm the only bloke who'd have them. And I'm not so sure I would take them either. Why should I? Maybe I should just dump them out in Central Park, and get some real use out of that nifty briefcase."

"We're here," Jack said. "And it looks like we're just in time. I take it Allison's not going to be here?" Jack asked with a smile.

Roger, correctly identifying Jack's comment as sarcasm, ignored it.

As Jack shut the door behind him, he scoured the crowd, looking for friendly, or at least familiar, faces.

"I see Pam, and Reg's son and daughter-in-law. But that's about it, aside from employees of the funeral home and the gravediggers. Must not have announced it in the *Times*."

"I think convention grants one funeral per lifetime," Roger responded. "And Reg used his up."

"Good thing they didn't start without us," Jack said. "Otherwise I'd have had them start over."

"Hello, Pam," Jack said as he slid in next to Reg's widow and gave her a hug.

He then hugged Meredith, Reg's daughter-in-law, and then Art, Reg's son.

"How many now?" he asked. "Kids, that is."

"Two," Art replied.

"It's really great to see you," Jack said. "Art, Meredith, you've met Roger? He was a good friend of your father's."

The two nodded that they knew Roger and then smiled pleasantly.

"We are gathered here today," the minister said, "as friends and family of Mr. Reginald Black. It is with sadness and sorrow that we pay our respects to this much-beloved man."

Jack was eager for the service to end. He had time constraints, plus he sensed that the less attention this drew, the safer everyone would be.

"The book of Ecclesiastes, chapter seven and verse two, tells us that 'It is better to go to the house of mourning, than to go to the house of feasting: for that is the end of all men; and the living will lay it to his heart.'"

"Do you see what I see?" Jack, pointing his thumb into the New York sky, asked Roger.

"Allison, no doubt," Roger responded in a hushed tone.

Jack was discreetly pointing at a helicopter drone hovering one thousand feet above the cemetery, directly above where they were standing.

"She's got someone close enough to monitor that camera," Jack said. "Even with a high-efficiency battery, it can't stay up much more than half an hour. Whoever is controlling it will probably crash it into some bushes and get the hell outta here."

"Better a Hero camera than a Hellfire missile," Roger chuckled.

"Definitely," Jack agreed.

"I cannot say that I knew Reg very well," the minister continued. "I was much closer to his widow, Pam, and their son. But every time I encountered Reg, he had kind words for me. And if there was one thing for which Reg was certain, it was his great love for his family and amazing loyalty to his friends."

"Do you see that Escalade parked to the southwest?" Jack asked Roger. "It's been there since before we drove up. I like it for the control vehicle."

"There's not been any activity around it," Roger agreed. "You could be right. If it's still there when this breaks up I might check it out."

Jack looked down at his watch and then whispered in Pam's ear, "I've got to leave here in about twenty minutes—I've got a plane to catch. I'll give you a call later."

Tears were tracking one behind another from behind the sunglasses that Pam Black wore, carrying with them the mascara she had put on that morning. She couldn't look up at Jack, but she did manage to acknowledge his words with a slow nod.

"I once read about a man who delivered a eulogy at the funeral of his close friend," the minister said. "He started off by reading the inscription on the deceased man's tombstone. After the man's name, it said 1950, followed by a dash, and then 2013. The speaker said that neither the date of birth nor the date of his death, were particularly important. What really mattered was the dash—what the man did during the timeframe represented by that dash.

"The man delivering the eulogy then looked out over those who were gathered graveside and said, 'You folks, the friends and family of my friend, you are privileged today to make of that dash whatever you wish—whatever seems important to you. That is what we are here for today—to celebrate the time our friend, or our beloved relative, spent on earth, for the great richness he added to our lives.

"I know for this man, the one who stands before you today, I am much richer because of the man whose life we are celebrating, that he lived and chose to call me his friend—"

Jack grabbed Roger's elbow and said, "Hey, buddy, take good care of these nice people. I gotta run. And take care of my brief-case as well. Take *very* good care of it."

Roger smiled and nodded as Jack quickly hugged Pam one more time and then headed to where he had spotted a car he suspected to be the one Kate was driving.

Chapter 50

Wednesday, 5:15 p.m. in Paris

At exactly five-fifteen that evening Jill called for a nurse. "Is Dr. Cartier still here?" she asked the nurse.

"I think so," she said. "I'll check for you."

Twenty minutes later Dr. Cartier came in.

"Mademoiselle Talbot, how are you doing?" he said. "You're looking better all the time."

"Dr. Cartier. My plane ticket is for tomorrow morning. I need to talk to my fiancé tonight. Can you do *anything* to move this along?"

"I'm sorry, but without the investigator's permission, we cannot release you."

"I know that. You said that before. So, when can I talk to the investigator to get this sorted out? I feel fine. I need to get back to my hotel and pack."

"I will call him again right now," he said.

"Let me talk to him."

"If I can reach him, I will do just that."

The doctor removed his cell phone from his scrub, along with the investigator's card, and dialed the number.

After a moment, he put his hand over the phone and told Jill he was getting the investigator's voicemail.

He then left this message, speaking slowly in English for Jill's benefit: "Investigator Pouliquen, this is Dr. Cartier from across the street. The patient we thought was Sylvia Bertrand is now awake. She told us her name is actually Jill—"

At that point, the voicemail was cut off because the doctor was speaking so slowly. He apologized and called the investigator back. This time he spoke rapidly in French.

When he was finished, he told Jill, "I left a message for Investigator Pouliquen. I explained that you needed to talk to him because your plane was scheduled to leave Paris tomorrow. That's the best I can do. I'm sure your fiancé has made other arrangements with the flight. Tomorrow we'll get this all sorted out. Perhaps the investigator will even see you yet tonight. But that is the best I can do right now. I am sorry."

Chapter 51

Wednesday, 5:25 p.m. in Paris

When I got back to the hotel after talking to the investigator, I logged onto my email account. First I wrote a note to Mr. Larson at the embassy, and then one to each of Jill's siblings. This time I personalized the notes—something I had not done before.

I then started packing. It was the most difficult thing I had ever done in my life.

First I pulled Jill's purple roller bag from the closet and opened it on the bed. I recalled how much she loved it—perhaps because, as a birthday present from her sisters, it epitomized their love for her. It was a little smaller than the one I used, yet she always seemed to fit everything into it. Usually, I packed the cameras and chargers in my larger case.

Even though I hated the process of packing, it felt like the right thing to do. It made me feel like I was expecting Jill to walk in the door at any minute, toss some gifts she had just bought onto the bed, and say, "Do you think we can squeeze these in?"

I left a little room in the large check-in suitcase just for that.

Under normal circumstances, I would do my best to keep the weight appropriately under fifty pounds for each of the check-in pieces. And because there was no weight limit on the carry-on pieces, I would try to pack small but heavier objects in them.

Right now, however, I was not going to worry about the weight of anything. If we were able to leave the next morning, we would just have to pay any additional fees.

Sadly, Jill had done no shopping, so we were heading back lighter than we had arrived.

I removed the remaining cash from the room safe, folded it, and slid it into my pocket. I did not count it, but I did notice that there were several one-hundred euro notes.

Our passports were in the safe as well. I sealed the envelope they were in and put them in my back pocket. I placed the printed flight schedule, with our confirmation number, in my back pocket as well. That emptied the safe.

Chapter 52

Wednesday, 9:00 p.m. in Paris

By nine p.m. I had everything packed except for my toothbrush and a mostly empty tube of toothpaste.

I crossed all the tasks off my list except for Love Lock.

I thought about heading down to the bridge, but it was too early. I wanted to spend a little time alone with only my thoughts for company—I would wait until all the tourists were back in their hotels.

Chapter 53

Thursday, 12:01 a.m. in Paris

At midnight Jill lay in her hospital bed crying. The investigator had not yet responded. She called for a nurse and asked if she could see her doctor again. The nurse told her he had left for the day and that he had the following day off.

Chapter 54

Thursday, 12:10 a.m. in Paris

I decided to take our luggage down to the front desk and have them store it for me. I did keep my MacBook in the room.

"Does that mean that they've located your fiancée?" the clerk asked enthusiastically.

I told him that the police had not yet found Jill, but that I wanted to get everything ready just in case. He understood. He could see that my eyes were swollen.

"Your shuttle is scheduled for eight a.m.," he said. "Do you still want it?"

"Oh yes," I replied. "If Jill gets here in time, we will still want to catch that flight."

"I see here that you have not yet paid the deposit, for the shuttle. Would you be able to do that now?"

"Sure," I replied, handing him the total amount for two passengers.

I then returned to the room and stretched out on my bed in the dark.

* * *

Jill could not sleep. But she had quit crying.

She had begun to develop a plan.

Chapter 55

Thursday,
12:42 a.m. in Paris

If she could somehow find some clothes, she would bolt.

If I run away, what is the worst thing that could happen? she reasoned. *I could be arrested. Then, at least, I might get to see that stupid investigator.*

She considered the room where nurses kept their street clothes. If she could locate that, she could steal whatever she needed.

Maybe I can get a look if I go out in the corridor, she thought.

She had been using the restroom on her own for the past two days, so she was beginning to get her walking legs back in condition.

She stopped first in the restroom and took a real look at herself in the mirror.

If Paul is going to see me tonight, I should clean up a bit, she thought.

However, she quickly determined that there was nothing she could do to fix herself up. First of all, she had no makeup. Besides, with all of her blonde hair shaved off to facilitate treatment of her head wound, all she could do was to cover her head with a hat or a scarf … and she had neither. She resolved that she could do nothing to improve her appearance.

She smiled at her reflection in the mirror and said aloud, "Well, Paul has never seen me like this before. This is going to be a real test of his love."

Just as she was preparing to leave the restroom, she heard some commotion going on just outside the restroom door.

"Sounds like they're bringing me a roommate—I had better get back in bed," she said with a big smile on her face.

"Mademoiselle Talbot," an unfamiliar nurse said. "Looks like you're going to have some company."

"That's great," Jill replied, carefully checking out where they were storing the new patient's clothing as she slid back into bed.

Chapter 56

Thursday,
1:00 a.m. in Paris

I looked at my computer on my way to the bathroom.

It's one a.m. I don't think I'm going to sleep tonight, I thought.

I brushed my teeth and put on my shoes. I took the envelope with the passports and laid it on the nightstand beside the bed. I pulled my investigator's tattered card out and stared at it. I smiled and spelled out his name aloud: "P-i-e-r-r-e T-i-f-f-e-n-e-a-u. I can't even pronounce most of the Metro stops, no way should I ever attempt to tackle that last name."

I laid the card on the passports and then put my coat on.

Chapter 57

Thursday,
1:03 a.m. in Paris

Pierre, bonsoir," Investigator Pouliquen said to his coun-
terpart, Pierre Tiffeneau, whom he had just called. "This
is Mickael. I'm sorry to call you so late, but I have some
fascinating news."

"Mickael, my friend. No problem. What have you got?"

"You know that case you've been working on—the one where you think the American murdered his fiancée?"

"Yes, go on."

"Well, she just turned up, *alive*. And get this. She is my Sylvia Bertrand. She is the one I told you about, the one who got robbed just outside Notre Dame. She just came out of her coma and informed her doctor that her name was really Jill Talbot. Can you beat that? Both of our cases solved with one call. Can you imagine the paperwork that's waiting for us?"

"Oh my God! And here I've been treating that poor man like a suspect."

"Well, he was a suspect. It's usually the husband or the fiancé. Hell, it's almost always the partner—husband or fiancé. You were just doing your job."

"Mickael, thank you for letting me know. Has the fiancé been informed?"

"No, I don't think so. I just listened to my voicemails, and the doctor had left me that message. I'm going over to the hospital right now and talk to her. I understand she is fully awake and feeling pretty good. Sometimes things just seem to work out in the end."

"I'm going to call the fiancé's hotel right now," Inspector Tiffeneau said, just before hanging up.

But just before the inspector could place his call, Paul left the hotel and headed toward the Love Lock Bridge. It was one-ten a.m.

Chapter 58

Thursday,
1:35 a.m. in Paris

At 1:35 a.m., I was standing on the east side of the Pont de l'Archevêché Love Lock Bridge, right where Jill and I had placed our lock.

I smiled when I thought about the shock registered on the desk clerk's face when I tipped him with a one-hundred euro note and asked him to please split it up with the others, that I really appreciated their sincere concern.

"Monsieur Martin, are you sure you want to do this?" he asked.

"Absolutely. You've all been great, and I might not get to see you again. My plane is leaving soon, you know."

"That is very generous," he said. "I will make sure it gets divided equally. Merci—thank you."

His phone was ringing, and he looked down at it.

"Thank you," I said as I left.

I knelt down, cradling our lock in both hands, and I read the inscription out loud: "Paul and Jill—forever lovers."

I then kissed it slowly and stood to my feet.

As I stood on the edge of the bridge, staring blindly into the lights of the city bouncing off the ripples of the water, I could not control my sadness.

When I caught myself melting, I forced the tears to stop by force-feeding random thoughts into my mind.

"I wonder how far downstream the keys to our lock drifted before catching on the bottom of the river?" I asked myself.

"That would depend on two things, primarily," I reasoned. "The depth of the river, and the speed of its flow."

There had been a lot of rain lately, and the Seine was unusually high. That caused the river to be a few feet deeper than usual, plus it sped up the flow.

"I would imagine that the flow of the river at the bottom would be substantially slower than it was at the surface," I calculated.

It was working. I had found a way to curtail my anguish.

"The static nature of the river's bed would slow the flow considerably. That means the keys would initially be briskly swept along for the first several meters. But then, their speed would decrease dramatically as they approached the riverbed.

"For any degree of accuracy, I would have to know the depth of the river. I'll have to think about that."

Chapter 59

Thursday, 1:37 a.m. in Paris

A t exactly 1:37 a.m., Jill saw her chance. The patient who was just admitted had been heavily sedated and was sound asleep.

Jill removed the new patient's clothes from the closet and rapidly put them on. Nothing fit, but she did not mind. She was shorter than most French women, so she rolled the blue jeans up and wrapped the black scarf neatly around her head.

She now had her total ensemble: shoes, pants, sweater, scarf, and a heavy woolen coat—she skipped the underwear. She took one last glance in the mirror and laughed out loud.

"Worst case scenario," she muttered, smiling as she left the room, "I get arrested—for bad taste."

She looked for a green "Running Man Sortie" sign. She spotted one at the end of the corridor and scurried toward it as rapidly as she could without breaking into a full run.

Jill knew her room was on the second floor, so as soon as she reached the bottom of the stairs, she headed for the first exit sign she saw.

She did not turn to face the night desk. She held up her right hand and waved. "Au revoir," she said loudly, by then almost running, while at the same time feigning that she was checking a watch.

Jill thought if she hurriedly rushed along, appearing as though she had someone waiting to pick her up, no one would question her.

She was right. Her leaving did go virtually undetected.

However, just as she was about to push open the final door, she encountered Investigator Mickael Pouliquen waiting on the other side of it.

Chapter 60

Thursday, 1:39 a.m. in Paris

The investigator had been waiting for the night nurse to open the locked door for him. Jill pushed the door open instead, and the investigator entered as she hurried south toward the Seine.

"Bonsoir, Mademoiselle," he said to her as she rushed past him. She did not acknowledge his greeting.

Of course, because they had not met, neither one of them recognized the other.

* * *

At 1:39 a.m., Jill was trying to get her bearings. She was just about to cross the Petit Point Bridge. She knew her way back to the hotel from Boulevard Saint-Michel, but she now found herself on Rue de la Cité.

She scrutinized the buildings on the other side of the Seine, looking for something familiar. That's when she spotted the Shakespeare & Company Bookstore. And directly to the west of the bookstore stood two of her favorite restaurants.

With the aid of those landmarks, Jill knew she could find her way back to her hotel.

Let's see, she thought. *This bridge takes me onto Rue Saint-Jacques, and it runs just east of Saint-Michel. I can take Saint-Jacques all the way down to Rue des Écoles, and the hotel is just west of there. No problem.*

As she stood waiting to cross Quai de Montebello, she remembered talking to Paul about the Shakespeare & Company Bookstore, and how they had wanted to spend half a day wandering through the stacks.

Before they had even contemplated their trip together, Jill had become fascinated with the history of the store.

The English language bookstore was opened by George Whitman in 1951. He patterned it after the original Shakespeare & Company Bookstore, founded in 1919 by Sylvia Beach, an American expatriate. The original store was located on Rue Dupuytren, and later moved it to Rue de l'Odeon in 1921. It remained there until it was closed by the Nazis in 1941.

The first store was noted for providing a place of meeting for such notables as Hemmingway, Ezra Pound, F. Scott Fitzgerald, Gertrude Stein, and numerous other intellectuals.

In 2011, George Whitman passed away, leaving the operation of the current store in the hands of his daughter, Sylvia Beach Whitman (whom he had aptly named after the founder). The store includes thirteen beds, which have served the needs of forty thousand young artists through the years.

Jill smiled for the first time in days as she stood at the intersection, staring at the store. *Guess I won't go through it on this trip*, she thought. *It will have to wait for our next visit to Paris—something to look forward to.*

Chapter 61

Thursday, 1:39 a.m. in Paris

At 1:39 a.m. I continued to calculate just how far downstream the keys to our lock could have traveled before settling to the bottom.

It was late winter—the Seine was high and muddy and its current *very* swift.

Whether it had to do with recent rainfall or just the time of the year, the river appeared to me to be much higher than usual. In fact, in places it had overflowed the walkway on the left bank.

I imagine the keys would have been carried quite some distance in a rapid flow like that, I thought. *And I think it's fairly deep. I've seen good-sized barges traveling up and down on it. It would have to be over fifteen feet deep. At least that's what I'd imagine.*

So, given the current and the depth, I'd guess the keys would have made it past the other side of the bridge—perhaps well past the other side.

In that split second, something inside of me presented the question of finding the keys as a full-blown challenge. I'm not sure about the driving force—whether it was fatigue, frustration, or desperation. Most likely it was the cumulative effect of all those negative factors cascading down on my psyche at the same time.

Whatever my motivations, self-destruction was not one of them. I truly believed I would find some keys—there had to have been enough of them down there. And, for the period of time that I would spend looking for them and getting back to safety, I would not be possessed by my failure to find Jill, nor would I be overwhelmed with the dread of my newly discovered disease.

I had done similar things in the past. In fact, when faced with a seemingly insurmountable challenge, I would often take out my aggressions in my parents' swimming pool. If I had gone to bed but couldn't sleep—perhaps because of a fight with a girlfriend or a poor score on an exam—sometime after midnight, long after my parents were asleep, I would jump out of bed and head to the pool.

Not wanting to bother with the thermal cover, I would take several long breaths and then do a dead drop into the deep end, between the cover and the edge of the pool. After touching the bottom, I would swim underwater all the way to the shallow end and, there, touch up.

I would frequently cover the length of the fifty-foot pool twice without coming up for air. I could swim very well and hold my breath forever.

By the time I was ready to get out, I had virtually forgotten about the problems that had so totally captivated me.

At that point, all I wanted to do was get warmed up and go back to bed. I'm not sure if it was substitution or misguided sublimation. But it worked.

So, on this night, I didn't just slide into the Seine—I dove in. If I was going to find the keys to our lock, I would have to make it to the bottom as quickly as possible.

Fifteen feet—not a problem, I reasoned.

Ostensibly my plan was to finger around on the bottom until I snagged some keys—actually any keys would do. And then I would swim over to the south concrete and stone bank of the river. I had already checked, and the level of the water was such that it came up to within inches of the walkway on the left bank—I could simply grab onto it. Even though my fingers would be cold and stiff, I would still be able to pull myself out.

I would then walk back to the hotel and take a hot shower. If nothing else, the exercise would have totally cleared my mind by giving me something else to think about.

Perhaps it would even provide me with a fresh approach to finding Jill.

In my mind, as I dove into the frigid waters of the Seine, I was simply diving beneath the pool cover, touching bottom, and then racing to the bank of the river. I was convinced that I would quite easily find a set of keys.

The problem was, the Seine was much deeper than I had presumed—possibly three times the depth of my parents' pool.

Plus, the icy temperature of the water was beyond anything I had ever experienced. And even though I was able to finally fight my way to the bottom, instead of finding keys, I discovered the bottom cluttered with an incredible amount of debris and thick soft silt.

After expending an enormous amount of energy, I concluded that the prospects of my finding any set of Love Lock keys was very slim at best. But I was prepared to spend as much time as possible looking—I would not give up easily. I was planning to snatch up the first small object my fingers touched and declare it to be *our* keys. I would then come back up, get my bearings, and swim to safety.

It was totally dark beneath the surface of the water. I tried opening my eyes, but the mud and pollution burned them so badly that I immediately closed them tightly and satisfied myself with just feeling my way along the bottom. Besides, at this point the only bearing critical to my success was up, and I had no difficulty determining which way that was.

While being fully clothed did help maintain my body temperature for a while, it substantially inhibited my ability to swim—particularly problematic were my heavy leather Timberland shoes.

I actually only touched the bottom one time, and that was with my initial dive. Every subsequent time I tried swimming back to it, the current just swept me along.

I did not want to give up. But after giving it everything I had, I began to sense failure.

Drowning is not an easy process—in fact, the human body has natural defense mechanisms that war powerfully against it. That's why water boarding is so effective.

Chapter 62

Thursday, 1:44 a.m. in Paris

Somewhere over the Atlantic, Jack was stretching out and trying to get comfortable. His plane was scheduled to land at CDG at 7:55 a.m., Paris time.

Would really be nice to get a little sleep, he thought. The six hours he was about to lose would be tough enough. Even if he could pick up a few hours before he arrived, he knew he could hold on for the rest of the day.

An hour earlier he had requested a few cookies and a glass of milk. Familiar with his body's metabolism, Jack knew that within thirty minutes, the initial sugar rush would have subsided, and he would be ready to get some sleep.

Finding an OnAir phone on the rear of the seat directly in front of him, he removed it from its mount and placed a call to Roger.

"Roger." He said. "This is Jack. And this call is costing me about five dollars a minute. So I'll make it short. I'll be landing in about six hours, and I just wanted to see if there was anything interesting going on before I took a little nap."

"Jack," Roger said. "You've not heard any news?"

"No. What's up?"

"There's been a plane crash in Upstate New York."

"Really?"

"And I did some checking. I'm really sorry, Jack, but you've got to know. The passenger list included Kate."

"Holy shit! Are you positive?"

"Jack, I made all the calls. Kate and twelve other people were on that plane. A state prosecutor, a female, was also on it."

"Oh my God! What else can you tell me? What do you know about survivors?"

"We don't have any word about that yet," Roger said. "Apparently witnesses saw some flames coming out of it. The pilot had some control, because he brought it down in a field—actually it was more like a marsh."

"It was a prop plane?" Jack asked.

"Turboprop. It was a small commuter plane. That works to her advantage, as far as surviving."

"How long before you will have something definitive?"

"No way to know," Roger said. "I can't call you till you get down. But you can call me as often as you want. I am really sorry, Jack. I will stay on top of this. Call me back as often as you wish."

Jack did not respond as he, with shaking hands, hung up the phone.

Chapter 63

Thursday, 1:44 a.m. in Paris

Even though my extremities were beginning to stiffen, my mind, at least for the moment, had never been clearer.

I started to accept the fact that I would not be able to rise to the surface of the river. My arms and legs felt foreign to me.

Drowning, I concluded, was now my only option.

However, I was discovering that drowning, while simple, was not going to be easy.

For instance, I found that you could not just intentionally inhale water. Your body won't let you do that. What happens is that you hold your breath for as long as you can and then, maybe, just a little longer.

Finally, it just begins to happen.

Initially, you try drinking the water—that your body will begrudgingly permit. But, as soon as that first mouthful of water hits your esophagus, you gag. And then you vomit.

That's when you first take water into your lungs—when you start gagging on the water you had been forced to swallow. That initial inhalation of water is just as involuntary as was the act of swallowing it, but far more powerful.

When my body first allowed some of the Seine into my throat, it burned even more than the water had hurt my eyes. Of course, I gagged, just like all drowners do.

I did not intentionally accept water into my lungs. In fact, I did my best to end my failed effort and swim to the surface.

But, at that point my fate was inevitable. My whole body, now growing limp from lack of oxygen and paralyzed by the frigid February waters of the Seine, could no longer respond to what my brain was asking it to do.

Perhaps part of my surprising weakness had to do with my heart condition. Maybe I was not getting enough blood pumped to my lungs. For whatever the reason, I was losing the fight. My body did not respond as I had expected, and my mind began to drift.

I could not respond to the chill that powerfully encompassed me.

Suddenly I felt the warmth of Jill's embrace. Her kiss was sweet and soft, and her eyes filled with the wonderment that had won my heart the day I took her hand as she walked off the stage at the music festival.

Ironically, while neither of us was aware of it, at that very moment our paths were crossing one last time.

My flaccid body had risen to the surface and was floating face down atop the swift Seine waters—at the precise instant Jill was crossing above me on the Petit Pont bridge.

Lifelessly I passed unnoticed beneath her feet.

Chapter 64

Thursday, 1:45 a.m. in Paris

As Jill reached the traffic light at Quai de Montebello, she smiled.

Paul is really going to be surprised to see me, she thought.

Even though there was not much traffic that early in the morning, she waited patiently for the signal to walk.

By the time it had turned green, several vehicles had stopped—

the closest one being a large delivery van. Carefully she stepped out into the street and headed for the hotel.

In her desire to get "home," Jill's still-healing brain totally failed to process the unique sound of an approaching emergency vehicle. Her eyes saw she had a green walk light—therefore she thought it was okay to cross.

As she stepped past the front of the delivery vehicle, she was immediately struck by an unmarked police car.

Of course, the plain-clothes officer driving the vehicle had properly activated the blue flashing light on his dash, and he had hit his siren. He had done all the things he was supposed to do.

And he was even proceeding through the intersection slowly.

Questions later surfaced as to why he had activated his emergency signals in the first place—he could not establish as fact that he was responding to his dispatch center. It was even suggested that he was on his way home and did not wish to wait for traffic.

Whatever his reason, the incident was quickly determined to have been an accident—no police culpability. Jill Talbot had wrongfully "fled" custody and simply failed to react to the siren in her attempt to escape.

The impact was minor. The driver of the police car had immediately applied his brakes. In fact, the bumper of his car had barely struck her legs. And were she not weak from the past four days in the hospital, she might have caught her balance.

But she didn't—she stumbled and fell. And when she did, the right side of her head smashed into the street. And she never moved again.

For a few seconds, however, her mind still functioned. She thought about her life, her sisters, and her happy days on Sugar

Island.

And, of course, she pictured Paul—forever the love of her life.

As always, he was smiling.

She smiled back—in her mind.

Chapter 65

Thursday, 7:55 a.m. in Paris

Jack's plane landed at CDG right on time. He had called Roger every half hour for updates on Kate's situation. His last call was just before he'd deplaned. There was still no word.

Once through immigration inspections, Jack activated his cell phone and called Roger again.

"Good news!" Roger blurted out. "Kate survived. She was transported to a hospital in Albany. She suffered some dings and minor burns, but it looks very good for her."

"And the other passengers?" Jack inquired. "She was traveling with a good friend of hers—a prosecutor."

"Not so good there," Roger said. "Only three people survived—Kate and two others. But, like I said, I have it on very good authority, Kate is okay. I would not give you false hope. In fact, from what I've learned, Kate actually dragged the other two survivors out of the burning plane. As it turned out, Jack, your daughter is a hero."

"I don't care about that—just as long as she's okay."

"Well, that I *do* know. Kate's gonna be fine."

Jack didn't say anything for a moment, and then he asked, "What caused it to go down? Anyone know that yet?"

"No one's talking officially until the NTSB has investigated," Roger said. "But off the record, it looks like it was sabotage. But don't quote me on that."

Chapter 66

Thursday, 8:00 a.m. in Paris

Right on time, the morning shuttle arrived at the hotel to take Paul and Jill to the airport.

It left empty.

Epilogue

Thursday, 11:09 a.m. in Paris

Jack arrived at the hotel where Paul and Jill were registered. He explained to the desk clerk that he was a private investigator from the US, and that he had been hired by the Sugar Island Talbot family to see if he could track down Jill Talbot, who had gone missing.

"Monsieur Handler," Gaspard Depardieu, the clerk at the desk said, after unsuccessfully trying to call their room. "They don't answer. And that's their luggage, over there," he continued, pointing at two large and three smaller pieces sitting off to the side. "We are aware of the problem with the Talbot woman. Here is the name of the Police Nationale investigator who is handling the case. I hope you can find her."

Depardieu wrote out the name of Claude Henreid on a piece of paper, along with the investigator's phone number.

"Police Nationale." Jack read aloud. "That is located on the other side of the Seine, near Notre Dame. Is that correct?"

"Oui, Monsieur," Depardieu replied.

"Merci," Jack said, excusing himself to flag down a taxi.

Jack entered the Police Nationale facility and asked for Claude Henreid. Almost immediately the very distinguished-looking investigator emerged and shook Jack's hand.

"My name is Jack Handler. I'm a private investigator from the US. The family of Jill Talbot has hired me to see what I can find out about her disappearance."

It took only a moment for the investigator to express his extreme sorrow regarding his office's failure to solve the case more quickly.

However, Investigator Henreid did not know that Jack had not yet learned about the death of both parties, and so he went on to express his deepest sympathies regarding what he called the "most unfortunate of outcomes—the death of both Jill Talbot and her fiancé, Paul Martin."

Jack was shocked.

"Dead!" Jack barked. "They're both *dead*?"

"Oui, Monsieur, I am so sorry. I assumed that you already knew about the tragedy. They died earlier today. Both accidental deaths."

"How certain are you as to the identity of the bodies?"

Jack was angry. His first inclination was to strike out at the nattily-dressed investigator. But he restrained himself.

"We are certain that Jill Talbot and Paul Martin are both deceased. We're *positive* about that."

Investigator Henreid continued to talk, but Jack paid no attention to what he was saying.

Finally, Jack dismissively waved off Henreid, turned away from him and headed toward the exit.

Investigator Henreid called out to him, "Monsieur Handler, there are many more details I should tell you."

Jack turned back to face Henreid. He paused for a moment, staring silently at the man, and then slowly walked to within a few inches of Investigator Henreid.

"Claude, right now I do not want to hear anything you have to say. I will come back once I have calmed down. I'm sorry, but all I feel like doing at this minute is to force you to take a swing at me.

"I've got some very difficult phone calls to make. And then some terribly involved arrangements. I will need to talk to you later, but not right now. I will tell you this. I spent my entire career working homicides. So I respect what you do. But when I see you the next time, I will seek from you only the information I need to get these two young people back to the States. So why don't you save your excuses for later, and for someone else. … I'm sure our embassy will have a lot of questions for you as this progresses. I suggest you get with your superiors, and take some time to get all your facts straight.

"Because, Claude, when all this shakes out, maybe a year down the road when I come back again, and I will come back, you'd better be able to explain yourself a little better. … In fact, you'd better be able to do one hell of a lot better job. … Don't take this as a threat,

Claude, just know that I'm not through with you yet."

Claude Henreid took a step backward and said. "As you wish, Monsieur Handler. I am very sorry about the way this turned out, and—"

Jack did not wait for him to finish his speech. He turned again, and this time he walked through the door and out onto the midday Paris street. It was cloudy, but not yet raining.

My God, Jack thought, walking only a dozen feet before stopping to ponder what had just transpired.

He rested one hand on a sign, and just stood there.

How could everything go this wrong?

Finally, he began to walk. Whether he intended to do so or not, his steps took him into Notre Dame Cathedral. He walked halfway to the altar and found an empty pew. There he knelt down and prayed.

* * *

The Inscrutable Puzzle?

In *Jack and the New York Death Mask* (first book in the "Getting to Know Jack" series) Jack's close friend, Reginald (Reg) Black, left this bloody cryptogram for Jack to find when he (Reg) was shot in a successful attempt to free Kate (Jack's daughter) from her Eastern European abductors.

At the time he discovered it (in Reg's blood-soaked trousers) Jack knew it was significant, and that Reg had intended it for him to find. However, the first night that it was in his possession it was stolen from Jack's hotel room. The culprit: two of former First Lady Allison Fulbright's operatives.

Fortunately, Jack had copied the puzzle, and taken an image of it before the theft.

Now Allison has reentered the picture, she has Reg's body exhumed from Calvary Cemetery in Queens, New York. Jack does not know her motivation, nor does Pam Black, Reg's widow.

Could it have something to do with the plaintext behind this cryptogram?

So far no one has been able to decipher the puzzle. Could it point to the location where Reg hid the one hundred million dollars in gold that he had received from Allison as payment for the assassination of a sitting president? Is that why Allison, before she discovered that Reg was not actually dead, was so adamant about digging him up? As of right now, we don't know where he hid the gold.

Some smart people have declared this puzzle to be inscrutable—unsolvable. But, we know better than that. There is no such thing as an unsolvable puzzle.

There is a key (of sorts) included with the puzzle in *Jack and the New York Death Mask.*

Cast of Characters
in the Getting to Know Jack Series

If you want to find out more about the series, then I would encourage you to check out the publisher's website (http://www. greenwichvillageink.com).

Jack: Jack is a good man, in his way. While it is true that he kills a lot of people, it can be argued that most (if not all) of them needed killing. Occasionally a somewhat sympathetic figure comes between Jack and his goal. When that happens, Jack's goal comes first. I think the word that best sums up Jack's persona might be "expeditor." He is outcome driven—he makes things turn out the way he wants them to turn out.

For instance, if you were a single mom and a bully was stealing your kid's lunch money, you could send "Uncle Jack" to school with little Billy. Uncle Jack would have a talk with the teachers and the principal. With Jack's help, the problem would be solved. But I would not recommend that you ask him how he accomplished it. You might not like what he tells you—if he even responds.

Jack is faithful to his friends and a great father to his daughter. He is also a dangerous and tenacious adversary when situations require it.

Jack Handler began his career as a law enforcement officer. He married a beautiful woman of Greek descent (Beth) while working as a police officer in Chicago. She was a concert violinist and the love of his life. If you were to ask Jack about it, he would quickly tell you he married above himself. So when she was killed by bullets intended for him, he admittedly grew bitter. Kate, their daughter, was barely a year old when her mother was gunned down.

As a single father trying to raise a daughter on his own, Jack soon found that he needed to make more money than his job paid. So he went back to college and got a degree in criminal justice. Soon he was promoted to the level of sergeant in the Chicago Police Homicide Division.

With the help of a friend, he then discovered that there was much more money to be earned in the private sector. At first he began moonlighting on private security jobs. Immediate success led him to take an early retirement and obtain his private investigator license.

Because of his special talents (obtained as a former Army Ranger) and his intense dedication to problem solving, many of Jack's jobs emerged from the darker side. While Jack did take on some of the more sketchy clients, he never accepted a project simply on the basis of financial gain—he always sought out the moral high ground. Unfortunately, all too often that moral high ground morphed into quicksand.

Jack is now pushing sixty, and he has all the physical problems common to a man that age. While it is true that he remains in amazing physical condition, of late he has begun to sense his limitations.

His biggest concern right now, however, is an impending IRS audit. He isn't totally confident that it will turn out okay.

His problems stem from the purchase of half-interest in a bar in Chicago nearly two decades earlier. His partner was one of his oldest and most trusted friends.

The principal reason he made the investment was to create a cover for his private security business.

Many, if not most, of his clients insisted on paying him in cash or with some other untraceable commodity. At first he tried getting rid of the cash by paying all of his bills with it. But even though he meticulously avoided credit cards and checks, the cash continued to accumulate.

It wasn't that he was in any sense averse to paying his fair share of taxes. The problem was that if he did deposit the cash into a checking account, and subsequently included it in his filings, he would then at some point be required to explain where it had come from.

He needed an acceptable method of laundering, and his buddy's bar seemed perfect.

But it did not work out as planned. Almost one year ago the IRS decided to audit the bar.

Jack hired one of his old customers, a disbarred attorney/CPA, to see if this shady character could get the books straightened out enough for Jack to survive the audit and avoid federal prison.

The accountant knew exactly how Jack earned his money and that the sale of a few bottles of Jack Daniels had little to do with it.

Even though his business partner and the CPA talked a good game about legitimacy, Jack still agonized about it when such thoughts barged through his mind.

Reg: In *Jack and the New York Death Mask (Death Mask)* Jack is recruited by his best friend, Reg (Reginald Black), to do a job without either man having any knowledge as to what that job might entail. Jack, out of loyalty to his friend, accepted the offer. The contract was ostensibly to assassinate a sitting president. However, instead of assisting the plot, Jack and Reg worked to thwart it. Most of this story takes place in New York City, but there are scenes in DC, Chicago, and Upstate New York. Reg is frequently mentioned throughout the series, as are Pam Black and Allison Fulbright. Pam Black is Reg's wife (he was shot at the end of *Death Mask*), and Allison is a former first lady. It was Allison who contracted Reg and Jack to assassinate the sitting president. She is currently on Pam Black's case, trying to get back the money she had paid Reg in the failed assassination scheme. Also, she still has aspirations on being president.

Kate: Kate, Jack's daughter and a New York homicide detective, is introduced early in this book. Kate is beautiful. She has her mother's olive complexion and green eyes. Her trim five-foot-eight frame, with her long auburn hair falling nicely on her broad shoulders, would seem more at home on the runway than in an interrogation room. But Kate is a seasoned New York homicide detective. In fact, she is thought by many to be on the fast track to the top—thanks in part to the unwavering support of her soon-to-retire boss, Captain Spencer.

Of course, her career was not hindered by her background in law. Graduating summa cum laude from Notre Dame at the age of twenty-one, she went on to Notre Dame Law School. She passed the Illinois Bar Exam immediately upon receiving her JD, and accepted a position at one of Chicago's most prestigious criminal law firms. While her future looked bright as a courtroom attorney, she hated defending "sleazebags."

One Saturday morning she called her father and invited him to meet her at what she knew to be his favorite coffee house. It was there, over a couple espressos, that she asked him what he thought about her taking a position with the New York Police Department. She was shocked when he immediately gave his blessing. "Kitty," he said, "you're a smart girl. I totally trust your judgment. You have to go where your heart leads. Just promise me one thing. Guarantee me that you will put me up whenever I want to visit. After all, you are my favorite daughter."

To this Kate replied with a chuckle, "Dad, I'm your only daughter. And you will always be welcome."

In *Murder on Sugar Island (Sugar)*, Jack and Kate team up to solve the murder of Alex, Jack's brother-in-law. This book takes place on Sugar Island, which is located in the northern part of Michigan's Upper Peninsula (just east of Sault Ste. Marie, MI).

A new main character is introduced in this book: Red, a red-headed thirteen-year-old who, besides being orphaned, cannot speak.

One other character of significance introduced in this book is Bill Green, the knowledgeable police officer who first appears in Joey's coffee shop. He assumes a major role in subsequent books of the series.

Red: Red has a number of outstanding characteristics. First of all, his ability to take care of himself in all situations. When his parents were killed in a fire, Red chose to live on his own instead of submitting to placement in foster care.

During the warmer months he lived in a hut he had pieced together from parts of abandoned homes, barns, and cottages, and he worked at a resort on Sugar Island. In the winter, he would take up residence in empty fishing cottages along the river.

Red's second outstanding characteristic is his loyalty. When put to the test, Red would rather sacrifice his life than see his friends hurt. In *Sugar,* Red works together with Jack and Kate to solve the mystery behind the killing of Jack's brother-in-law Alex. Alex was the owner of the resort where Red worked, and he shared a very significant relationship with the boy.

The third thing about Red that makes him stand out is his inability to speak. As the result of a traumatic event in his life, his voice box was damaged, resulting in his disability. Before Jack and Kate entered his life, Red communicated only through an improvised sign system, and various grunts.

When Kate introduced him to a cell phone, and texting, Red's life changed dramatically.

In *Superior Peril (Peril)* and *Superior Intrigue (Intrigue),* all of the above characters play major roles. Plus there are some new colorful characters introduced in those two books. One of them is Robby, Red's best friend.

In this book, *Sugar Island girl—Missing in Paris (Missing),* the fifth book of the series, Jack and Kate are again the main characters, with appearances by Roger and Captain Spencer. While Robby and Red take a break in this book, they do come back in future volumes of the "Getting to Know Jack series."

Two new characters emerge in *Missing.* They are Paul Martin and Jill Talbot.

The sixth book of the series is due out in June of 2014. The title of that book is *Wealthy Street Murders (Wealthy Street).* In this book Jack and Kate work with Red and Robby to solve a series of murders. Mrs. Fletcher, part-time caretaker at Kate's resort on Sugar Island, plays a more prominent role. *Wealthy Street* is set in Grand Rapids, MI.

Made in the USA
Middletown, DE
02 October 2020